Sub Rosa

SUB ROSA

An Egidio Manfredi Mystery

Ralph [M.] McInerny

Five Star • Waterville, Maine

This novel is a work of fiction. Names, characters, places, and incidents are either the product of the author's imagination, or, if real, used fictitiously.

Five Star First Edition Mystery Series.

Published in 2001 in conjunction with Tekno-Books and Ed Gorman.

Set in 11 pt. Plantin by Rick Gundberg.

Printed in the United States on permanent paper.

Library of Congress Cataloging-in-Publication Data

McInerny, Ralph M.
    Sub Rosa : an Egidio Manfredi mystery / Ralph McInerny.
        p. cm. — (Five Star first edition mystery series)
    ISBN 0-7862-3559-4 (hc : alk. paper)
    1. Police — Ohio — Fiction. 2. Women novelists — Fiction.
3. Lottery winners — Fiction. 4. Kidnapping — Fiction. 5. Aged
men — Fiction. 6. Ohio — Fiction. I. Title. II. Series.
PS3563.A31166 S8 2001
    813'.54—dc21   2001045052

For George Martin
Southern discomforter

Prologue

One change that Manfredi approved of was that you can't make a police officer retire. Of course most cops got out as soon as they could, twenty years and a pension, why not? For Manfredi, that would have meant getting another job or listening to Theresa all day. And so he stayed on, the dean of the Fort Elbow, Ohio Police Department.

But no law could make a department like it when a detective persists in staying active. Various ploys had been tried to make Manfredi regard the green pastures of retirement as attractive. They had put him in an out of the way office with the lucious Gloria, hoping to eject him on a morals charge, but that hadn't worked. Manfredi wasn't going to pop for the necessary Viagra and besides he respected Gloria and vice versa. So they gave him Noonan as an assistant, putting him at a desk in the same room as Gloria. That had been a near thing.

There are two kinds of bad partner. Those who talk a lot and those who talk more than a lot. Noonan was the second kind. He couldn't shut up. He had a half-ass education and had a way of treating Gloria and Manfredi as if they were retarded. Finally, asking him to repeat things had done the trick.

"Say that again," Manfredi would urge Noonan.

"One more time," Gloria said, saying one word at a time,

7

sounding like Ella Fitzgerald.

At first Noonan was flattered, then he got annoyed. Then he began to stammer. He searched for words. He fell silent. He fled upstairs to the Appointments Board.

Manfredi's suggestion was Missing Persons, and that is what Noonan got. The chief, reminded that Manfredi was still amongst them, put him back in Homicide where he belonged.

"Forget my rank," Manfredi said. He was a captain.

"You taking a pay cut too?"

"Ha."

The chief made fifty-six thousand a year, about what a mediocre minor league pitcher gets for going six innings. As for captains' salaries, don't ask. But Manfredi was glad to be back in Homicide with the gore, violence, and cadavers. It made longevity meaningful. Not that it was work. At the moment, there seemed to be more missing persons than homicides.

Part One

SNATCH

—

1

The walls of the room in which she wrote were paneled with cork and there was a thick carpet on the floor. Behind closed blinds, wearing earplugs, comfy in an extra large jogging suit, Rosa Subiaco sat daily before her computer writing under a platoon of pen names the jumbo novels that had earned her a vast and loyal readership from coast to coast.

Writing took her out of herself, out of her cluttered house, out of her two hundred-pound body into a world of fragile beauty and fierce male desire not to be denied. She was now well into the third novel in her saga about the building of the Erie Canal and the men and women whose lives had become entangled in a web of lust and greed and westward expansion. From the basement rose a constant monotonous banging on a pipe, penetrating her defenses, disturbing her concentration.

Her acute senses, her vulnerable emotions, were the basis of her literary success. A psychic counselor had pronounced Rosa's hearing to be as keen as an animal's, an equivocal compliment, but it was true.

"Your aura is polychrome, a rainbow of dazzling light."

The aurora borealis? Hector, her counselor, was a boring borealis as far as Rosa was concerned. She could not make up her mind whether Hector was a conscious or unconscious fake.

"How does my mind appear to you?"

He looked around, as if for a simile. His face lit up. "Like your computer screen."

"Read it."

He closed his eyes and frowned. He rubbed his forehead. "I am getting interference." He opened his eyes. "You have been writing another story."

"Can you read it there?"

"It is not like thoughts."

"Read my thoughts."

He looked deeply into her eyes, his face moved to the right, his chin dipped, his eyes remained locked with hers.

"Naughty, naughty," he whispered.

They were naughty in a bedroom on the first floor, to save her the trouble of climbing stairs.

The following night she drove him to a bridge spanning the Prune River and hoisted him onto the railing. When she was tying the concrete block to his ankles, a car approached, but she was blocked from view by her parked van. It went on by and Rosa completed her task. She eased Hector forward and soon the weight of his body slowly lifted the concrete block from the sidewalk. But the block caught on the railing and Hector hung suspended in the dark until, with a gloved hand, Rosa tipped the block over the railing. The silence of his fall seemed as audible as the sound the body made when it entered the water.

That had been two, no, three years ago. Hector was the second man she had dumped into the river after taking such pleasure as he could afford. She was motivated by the radical change that took place in Hector once his desire had been satisfied. In the blur of lust she had been invisible, but afterward a cold eye was turned on her and she knew what that cold eye saw. Had he been in bed with that? She was barely five feet tall, shapeless and obese, her features scrunched together under the pressure of facial fat. She had no illusions about herself. It was her fancy that she belonged to another species, bearing only a superficial resemblance to humans. Yet humans fascinated her, their flaws and antics attractive because she could not take part. Sometimes she thought she was more than human and that, even under the best of conditions, she could not be happy as a mortal woman.

In her sprawling novels she tracked her heroines from bed to bed, throwing them into sinewy arms and knowing a vicarious thrill when they gave themselves heedlessly to handsome strangers. Where did these wild stories come from? Readers from coast to coast devoured them. But Rosa's personal experience of men was another thing.

She stopped her fat little fingers from flying over the computer keyboard and closed her eyes impatiently. From below the desperate clinking noise continued, the sound of metal against metal. Julius had found something else with which to hit the water pipe. If this were not her writing time, she might have been amused. She did admire his persistence. There had even been times when she thought he might be a keeper, but Julius's days were numbered.

His longevity was due to the fact that he could not see a thing without his glasses, almost literally. For Julius she was merely an amorphous shape, warm flesh in which he had found an unlooked-for consolation. She had come upon him groping about in the supermarket parking lot. After watching him crouch and pat the asphalt with his hand, describing an ever widening circle, she asked him if she could help.

"I've lost my glasses."

The glasses were just a foot beyond the patted perimeter of his searching hand. Rosa picked them up and put them in her pocket.

"What do they look like?"

She stayed with him when it became clear that he was alone and that he could not drive without his glasses.

"I shouldn't drive with them for that matter, but how else can I get to the store?"

"If you were wearing them, how did you lose them?"

The bows were loose, when he bent over to put the groceries in his car, they had slipped off his head.

"I heard them hit. Can't you see them?"

"No. You could go into Osco's and buy a cheap pair."

He laughed. He had a nice smile. Think of him as blind, blind and handsome. He was in his fifties. The over the counter glasses sold in drug stores were not nearly powerful enough to enable him to see.

"I am legally blind."

And drove a car! She asked if she could call someone. "Your wife?"

"I no longer have a wife."

"I'm sorry."

"Don't be. She left me. I can't say that I blame her."

There were no children either. She told him her name and again he laughed.

"Is it funny?"

"My wife used to read steamy novels by a Rosa Charrin. She read them aloud."

Rosa Charrin was one of her pseudonyms. "Look, I don't see your glasses anywhere. Why don't I give you a ride."

His name was Julius Sweeney and he had been a patent attorney as long as his eyes held out. Now he was on social security and had a pension from his firm. That had been in another city. They had moved here to Fort Elbow, Ohio when his handicap was complete because this was where his wife had grown up.

14

"And then she left you."

"I am not an easy person to live with."

"Who is?"

And so it began. She took him home, she babied and pampered him, and affection had been so rare in his life of late that he was putty in her hands. The fact that he could not see her gave Rosa a confidence she had never felt with a man before. She persuaded him to stay by promising him that she would go to his eye doctor and get a prescription for new glasses. Meanwhile he could relax. That was when she took him to the basement where there was a cot and a little bathroom. He drank the warm milk laced with sleeping tablets and within minutes was fast asleep. Standing there, looking at him, Rosa began to dream of how convenient it would be to keep him here, as a kind of pet, a man available when the urge was on her.

Growing up in Toledo she had been all but invisible to boys, despite her girth, but plain girls liked to be seen with her since the contrast made them desirable. After high school, she had gone to business school and learned how to operate a computer. She easily found a job with a local realtor, who put her in a private office. She was flattered until she realized she was being kept out of sight of clients. With her friend Jane she frequented the Lotus Lanes bowling alley where minors were served beer and there were always boys on the prowl. As the night progressed and the beer took its toll, Jane always landed them dates of a sort. This meant going off and parking by the river and allowing the boy to grope his way to solitary satisfaction. Afterward, he would fall asleep and Rosa tried not to monitor what Jane was up to in the back seat. Jane was anxious to acquire sexual experience but what she acquired was a child. The boy offered to pay for an abortion and Jane was tempted, but she was more tempted by the thought of having her child. She went off to Atlanta to become a single mother and Rosa began to write. Transposing those sweaty evenings by the river into a romantic key, she began to write of Jane's irresistible attraction for men. Her imagination surprised her at first and she did not immediately know why she was writing the stories that came so easily. A writing club at the library put her on the path to prolific and more or less anonymous fame. Her family name was Subiaco, but she published her first romantic novel under a pen name. As Rosa Charrin she became well established, she acquired an agent, she quit her job and moved to Fort Elbow. Until Hector she had lived like a nun, but her authority when she sat at her computer gave her confidence with men, confidence but without allusions. She knew what men wanted, but then she knew what she wanted too. She used her conquests like Kleenex, disposable after use. Julius was a departure but he was becoming an annoyance, making that incessant noise in the basement by banging his keys against a pipe.

She drove him to the West Toledo mall where she had found him and left him there.

2

There were pictures of Grandpa in the albums on the shelves beside the fireplace, albums Lucy's mother had compiled. There were even several cassettes of home movies that Lucy only dared play when her Aunt Edna and Uncle Fred were out. How strange it was to see Grandpa acting like anyone else. You could see how everyone looked up to him. There was one sequence in which her mother smiled so sweetly at him and Grandpa smiled back, so proud of his daughter. Lucy would freeze the film, then rewind it, playing it over and over again. She showed it to Grandpa but he had no reaction at all. He did not respond to the image of Lucy's mother nor did he seem to recognize on the screen the man he had been before his mind began to go.

He had not been too bad when Lucy's mother talked him into living with them. There was only her and Lucy then. How relieved the relatives were, particularly Aunt Edna and Uncle Fred.

"Thank God you can afford it," Edna said.

"A father always prefers a daughter," Fred added. Grandpa was his mother's brother. Whatever the relationship, probably cousin, they became aunt and uncle.

That had changed the life Lucy and her mother lived, the house was different with Grandpa there, but Lucy noticed that her mother seemed younger. At least while Grandpa still

17

knew who she was. Aunt Edna was right, they could afford it. Lucy's father had been killed long ago in Vietnam and there was a pension plus the enormous insurance policy he had taken on his life.

"The premiums were so high!" her mother said, her voice full of the sense that her father had some premonition that he would not come back to them. Sometimes it bothered Lucy that she felt closer to Grandpa than to her father. But her father had been only a memory most of her life while Grandpa was the father her mother loved.

Things kept right on changing after Grandpa moved in. Edna and Fred came by from time to time, not so much to see Grandpa, it seemed, as to criticize the way Lucy's mother took care of him.

"He should get more exercise."

"Hasn't he lost weight?"

Grandpa had lost his appetite along with his memory and it was like feeding a baby getting him to eat. And then, suddenly, Lucy's mother became ill with cancer and the progress of the disease was swift. The last thing her mother said to her was, "Look after Grandpa."

She had not needed to be told that. Grandpa was all she had now and it didn't bother her that he was so helpless. Sometimes he would be gripped with uncaused fears and then Lucy was especially attentive. He needed her more than she needed him. He did not know who he was or who he had been and Lucy's great fear was that he too would die and she would be left entirely alone. That fear made her receptive when Edna and Fred said they were moving in with her. They would leave their home and friends in Toledo and move to Fort Elbow to live with Lucy and Grandpa.

"Legally I suppose we are your guardians."

"I am twenty-one."

"I meant we are the only family you have."

There was no mortgage on the house and her father's army pension was more than enough to support her, pay the taxes and keep the place in good repair.

"Why don't we let Fred look after things," Edna said after she had asked to see the first pension check that arrived soon after her aunt and uncle moved in. They gave up the lease on their apartment. Of course they did not pay rent to live in the house and there was more than enough money for them all. Lucy did not tell Aunt Edna about the insurance money, which was managed for her by Alex Schuler, a lawyer who had been a boyhood friend of her father and said he felt guilty that his bad leg had kept him out of the service. Managing the money was a patriotic duty. He had looked thoughtful when she told him about her aunt and uncle.

"Have you told them of your investments?"

"Should I?"

"Maybe not."

Of course he was a lawyer and naturally suspicious but Lucy took his suggestion. It seemed all the wiser when Fred took over the management of the house and had her sign a paper that authorized him to put the checks in an account Lucy nominally shared with Fred and Edna. Still, it was nice not to have to worry about managing things. There was a special provision for her education, so she continued at the Fort Elbow campus of the University of Ohio where she majored in English.

"English," Aunt Edna said. "What good is that?"

"I like it."

Since the fund had to be used for education, Edna finally accepted what she clearly thought was a waste of time. She had suggested that Lucy should get a job, to help out.

"After I graduate. I want to teach."

But it was Grandpa who became the principal object of Edna's discontent.

"He should have professional care."

"But I want to take care of him."

"He is your responsibility."

Meaning neither Edna nor Fred would share the responsibility with her. That was just as well. Grandpa did not like Edna. Often when Lucy came home from class, her grandfather would be lost in frightened gloom. He only perked up when Lucy took him out. He particularly liked the mall.

3

Edna's friends were impressed by her generosity, looking after Fred's niece and the old man with Alzheimer's. Imagine, actually leaving Toledo and beginning a new life in Fort Elbow.

"What are relatives for?"

"But you and Fred had such a good life here!"

Edna would close her eyes and shake her head, as if she were warding off temptation. She liked the thought that she and Fred had made a great sacrifice, giving up their apartment and moving to Fort Elbow to live with Lucy and Grandpa. Fred commuted to Toledo and continued at Thompsons, the realty office where he had been employed, a mediocre salesman who did not instill confidence in prospective buyers. Edna had tried to put some steel into him, some confidence, but without success. She knew she could sell igloos to Eskimos if she gave it half a try.

"Why don't you then?"

"You said you didn't want a wife who worked."

"When did I say that?"

"Don't tell me you're losing your memory too."

That had been inspired. It became one of Fred's anxieties that he would end up like Grandpa. If he ever did, Edna would not attempt to take care of him. That was a job for professionals. Meanwhile, the new assured income, was a welcome change. It affected Fred too, and he began to be a more effective salesman. Finally, after fifteen years of marriage, their life together was more pleasant. If Edna had ever felt guilt about the amount of time she spent playing bridge, she was no longer burdened with it. Her cousin-in-law had become their posthumous provider. The only fly in the ointment was his doddering uncle.

She was in a receptive mood when the story appeared in the paper about the blind man who had been found wandering around the parking lot of a mall in West Toledo. It was a pathetic story, played for all the pathos it contained, but Edna read it with unemotional concentration. The man claimed he had been kidnapped from that very mall weeks before and it turned out that his automobile had been towed away to the police garage after it had been standing there for days. A blind man's car? But Edna's mind was filled with the image of that helpless man, wandering around until he had been asked what he was looking for.

"My glasses."

Only gradually did it come out that he had been kidnapped. His glasses were found in his jacket pocket. There was a photograph of him as he put them on and looked around at a suddenly visible world.

He might have been Grandpa Yates.

4

Alex Schuler had grown up in Fort Elbow, an introspective
youth with a passion for the Civil War. By tenth grade he could
write out from memory the major dates of the war, the decisive
battles, from Charleston to the surrender at Appomattox Court
House. He had been a child in World War II and still in high
school when war in Korea limped to a truce. At night he would
lie awake, cursing his fate that he had missed the opportunity for
heroism. He imagined fighting and dying in a heroic way. His
book review of Stephen Crane's *The Red Badge of Courage* had
been unrelentingly severe. How could an author write so cyni-
cally of war? And then came Vietnam.

"This is our chance," Don Yates had said.

"We may not be drafted."

"Drafted. I am going to enlist."

Alex fell ill on the day Don went down to the Marine
Corps recruiting office in Toledo and volunteered. Alex had
been accepted by the University of Ohio at Fort Elbow law
school and his parents urged him to enter now.

"Don has enlisted."

"The war can wait. Get your law degree and apply for a
commission."

It helped to think of law school as his version of ROTC.
Vivian let him read the letters that Don wrote. He squired her
about, as good as a brother since he and Don were such

friends. In his third year of law school, he stood at the open garage door while his father prepared to back the car out of the garage. When he put out his foot and felt the first pressure of the tire on his foot, he was almost disappointed at how easy it was, but then the excruciating pain began and he screamed. His father stopped the car so that the tire rested on his foot. When he got out of the car and saw what he had done, he scrambled behind the wheel and in his excitement went forward, and Alex passed out.

His parents hovered over him in the hospital. Vivian came to see him, her face a mask of pain as if she were looking at Don rather than just Alex. Alex wept genuine tears, his remorse real.

"I can never join him now," he sobbed, and Vivian took him in her arms. A month later the wire came, telling her that her husband had died a hero's death in Vietnam.

"It could have been you," his father whispered, when he heard the news.

That had been Alex's first thought. It should have been him. He was a coward. He had deliberately ruined his foot to stay out of harm's way. But there was more. While Don had been facing danger in Vietnam, Alex had been safe in Fort Elbow, visiting with Vivian.

He came to see that he loved Vivian, but at the same time knew that there was nothing he could do about it. It would be a worse betrayal to seek to replace Don with his wife and daughter. What he could do is see that they were never in want. He had offered his services as financial advisor when the insurance money came, and Vivian was happy to have such a trusted friend to look out for her and little Lucy.

His handicap was taken for the reason that he had never married, but he had taken a private vow of celibacy to make up to Don for his own cowardice. There had been moments when Vivian's response to his supposed selfless generosity might have led to something more, but it was always Alex who had prevented it. Don had never seemed so present while he was still alive, and Alex felt his dead friend's eyes upon him always. He assured the ghost that he had nothing to fear. There were some deeds so low not even he could perform them.

The insurance money grew into a near fortune under his tutelage. It gave him pleasure that he had made Don's widow far wealthier than he himself was. They reached an age that was forever denied Don, he and Vivian, and little Lucy became a girl and then a young woman. When Vivian was diagnosed with cancer, Alex felt that she was being punished for his own deficiencies. Now there was only Lucy and she regarded him as a father.

"She's your aunt?" Alex asked when Vivian had told him of Edna.

"No, Lucy's. Sort of."

"Then she is the sister of Don's cousin?"

"That's it."

"What right does she have to criticize the way you are caring for him?"

"She's just concerned."

She sounded like a bitch to Alex, and when he met her, the estimate was confirmed. Fred the husband was a wimp, grinning and nodding at whatever his wife said, always walking a step or two behind her. Alex had been of two minds when Vivian said she was going to bring her father-in-law in her home. He was in the first stages of Alzheimer's and she intended to do what she was sure Don would have done.

"Are you sure?"

"You know he would have."

Don had assumed mythical status for her as well. Did she

25

really remember him? The story of how he had died trying to save his buddies on patrol was one she loved to tell, and Alex enjoyed her telling it because of the pain listening to it gave him. Yes, she was right. Don would have brought his diminished father under his own roof to care for him. Alex had come to the house with complete information on how she might commit the old man to a nursing home but he never took the papers from his briefcase. He felt ashamed for having brought them. And then Vivian fell ill.

"There are two consolations, Alex. One is that I know you will look after Lucy."

"Of course I will." He dreaded asking her what the other reason was, but he did.

"I will be with Don soon."

All too soon, as it happened. The cancer reduced a beautiful woman to a scarecrow, the treatment robbed her of her hair, but the smile, despite her skeletal face was unchanged. Her bright eyes seemed full of the hope that she would soon be reunited with Don. Alex promised that he would be a father to Lucy.

"Don't do it," he advised Lucy when she told him her aunt and uncle proposed moving from Toledo and living with her in Fort Elbow.

"I wish you could live with us."

Dear God, how he loved the child, only she wasn't a child anymore. Her manner with him was one of total trust and he would kill himself before he betrayed it. She might have been her mother when she was young, when he and Don had been young, and there were times when the thought came that a generation had intervened, that life was passing him by. So be it. It was the fate he deserved. He dropped his objections to Edna and Fred moving in with her and Grandpa.

The old man was healthy, despite his terrible affliction,

and it occurred to Alex that their presence in the house was Lucy's chance to live a life of her own. Now she would not be the sole guardian of her grandfather and all life's possibilities could open up for her.

5

It was reading Willa Cather that made Lucy decide to major in English; the novel *Lucy Gayheart* stirred up in her the thought of becoming a writer. Nick, a fellow in her American literature course, told her about the phenomenally prolific author who lived in Fort Elbow.

"A real hack. She can write a novel in a month."

Lucy tried to imagine Willa Cather writing a novel in a month. "Have you read any of them?"

Nick made a face. They were exactly the same height and it felt comfortable looking him in the eye. It was like a vacation to talk with someone who didn't know anything about her, didn't know that she had lost her father and then that her mother died and that she lived with her grandfather who had Alzheimer's and an aunt and uncle she did not like. Meeting someone was so strange, each person trailing a whole history that will only become known to the other gradually. Was it only at the beginning that it was this exciting? Lucy felt like Eve before Original Sin talking with Nick.

"They're women's novels."

"Is that a type?"

He laughed. "You're right. Most readers are women, so I guess every writer is writing for them."

"Is that what you want to do?"

"Write for women?" He had become wary and Lucy had

the sense that she had discovered his secret.

"I want to be a writer like Willa Cather," she said.

His wariness was gone. "No kidding. She was a hack at first."

"She was not!"

"She worked for a slick magazine."

"*McClure's*."

"So you know about that."

There was little about Willa Cather she didn't know. She had read the biographies that went on about what a tomboy Willa had been, but that was her father, dressing her like a boy when he took her to Europe. And so what if she had never married. Lucy had been ready to forego marriage herself, if she could be a writer like Willa Cather, but that thought drifted away as she got to know Nick better. The next semester, when she showed up on the first day of her creative writing course, there he was. A moment's awkwardness and then he smiled. They sat next to one another while the teacher, a woman who might have been eighty, taught them as if nothing had changed in writing and publishing for fifty years.

"Ask her if she knew Willa Cather," Nick wrote on the note he slipped to her.

"I'm afraid to," she answered.

On no basis whatsoever, they came to think of themselves as sophisticated moderns who were amused by their old-fashioned teacher. And there were times when Miss McManus seemed to be speaking directly to their skepticism about her knowledgeability.

"A story is what Aristotle said it was," Miss McManus told them with conviction. "Fads and fashions change, but not what a story is."

She spent that session discussing Aristotle's *Poetics*, which was unusual. As a rule, class sessions were taken up criticizing the work of students, in the course of which Miss McManus made comments and suggestions. The day she talked about Aristotle they could see what had lain behind her editorial remarks. And what she said made sense.

"A story must have a beginning, a middle and an end," Nick would quote to Lucy, half kiddingly, but she knew how impressed he had been.

"The plot is the soul of the story," she echoed.

For weeks their attitude toward the class changed, and then one day, bored, Nick asked Miss McManus what she thought of Rosa Charrin.

"Is she a writer?"

"The most prolific writer in the greater Fort Elbow metropolitan area."

"What has she written?"

Lucy nudged Nick, wishing he would stop teasing Miss McManus, because that is what he was doing. Only Miss McManus refused to be teased.

"Which of her novels is your favorite?"

"Oh, I've never read any of them."

"Ah."

"They're romance novels."

"And how would you define a romance novel?"

"Well, there's a woman in distress and people tormenting her and then along comes a man who rescues her."

"That could describe any number of novels. Great novels."

"She's a native of Toledo," Nick said lamely. "I'm from there too."

Lucy told him later it served him right, trying to embarrass that lovely old woman.

"Well, I didn't succeed."

"I liked the story we critiqued today."

His face lit up and he could not keep the smile from his lips. "It was mine."

"Really? It was wonderful." Impulsively she leaned toward him and kissed his cheek.

"Charles de Gaulle would have kissed both cheeks."

"He couldn't see too well."

"Would you like to kiss me on the veranda?"

The Three Amigos was one of his favorite films. He had a taste for farce and mad comedy. Yet his story had been a soulful portrait of a boy growing up in a home without a mother. He had been told that his mother had died but the story turned on the moment when he learned that she had abandoned her family. This Joycean epiphany led to the closing paragraph in which the boy pores over a map of the country, putting his finger down, here, now there, imagining that he could locate the mother he had never known.

"I expected her to say it had no plot."

"Oh, it is a perfect story."

"Hey." But he loved it. After a moment, smile gone but looking her directly in the eye the way she liked, he said, "It's my own story."

From that moment she knew that someday she would be able to tell him all about her life.

It was Aunt Edna who told Lucy that the local author who wrote under the name of Rosa Charrin, among others, would be speaking about her writing at the library in Toledo.

"What's she like?"

"I've never met her." Aunt Edna seemed almost indignant at the suggestion. In his chair, Uncle Fred's face appeared briefly over the newspaper he was reading and then set like the sun.

"We should go hear her."

"Whatever for?"

"But you're always reading her books," Fred said.

A flush fanned over Aunt Edna's face and half a dozen replies seemed to form in her mind only to be rejected. In the end she ignored the remark.

"Fred, will you stop rattling that paper!"

Lucy asked Nick if he meant to hear Rosa Charrin speak.

"How did you hear of it?"

"My aunt. She used to live in Toledo. My uncle commutes and brings home the local paper."

"Would you like to go?"

And so their first date, if you could call it that, was attending a talk by Rosa Subiaco, a.k.a. Rosa Charrin, et al.

6

It was Rosa's first agent Franklin Leach who had convinced her to blow her cover and admit that she was the author of the novels that were becoming so popular with millions of readers of paperback originals.

"I don't look like Rosa Charrin," she told him over the phone. They had never met in person.

"What do you mean?"

"I'm ugly."

He thought about it, humming as he did. "That could work. You ever see a picture of Lilian Hellman?"

"She looked like a movie actress compared to me."

"You're exaggerating."

This debate went on for months and then one day his flight was diverted and he called her from the Fort Elbow airport. Rosa agreed to come see him. That seemed as good a way as any to put an end to his campaign to have her reveal the woman behind the pseudonyms. She was not prepared for the little man hardly taller than herself waiting for her in the bar. He got up and they stared at one another for a full minute before he opened his arms and gathered her to him. The fraternity of freaks.

He became half drunk before they left the airport bar. In her van he said, "A shower and a little nap and I'll be as good as new."

"When does your flight leave?"

He slapped her playfully on the thigh. "You're the pilot."

She signed him into an airport motel and left a note for him. The thought of tumbling about on the king-sized bed in his suite was tempting, but Rosa was afraid that if she slept with him she would have to kill him, and he was a good agent. By phone, a week later, she agreed to let the publisher prepare a release on the woman behind the writer.

The photographs were so flattering that for a fleeting moment Rosa actually thought she looked like that. The main shot was taken very close, and Rosa did have a halfway interesting face. Her eyes looked as if there were millions of stories lying just behind them, which was probably true. The picture showing her at her desk was so set up that Rosa might have been six feet tall. In the year that followed, her sales tripled and continued to rise.

But Rosa resolutely refused all suggestions that she show up at bookstores or writers' conventions to sign books. Invitations to speak were dropped unread into the wastebasket. Rosa knew that her success could never survive showing what she really looked like. Besides, she preferred anonymity. The publicity photographs were as good as a disguise, they were so unlike her. So she had the advantages of revelation with none of the disadvantages. She told Franklin he was a genius.

"I know."

"I'm sorry I said it."

"Did you doubt me? I told you what the results would be."

"That was before we met."

"I have only the haziest memory of that."

"You shouldn't drink."

"I don't. I quit. I go to meetings where I bore and am bored by other former drunks. It's enough to drive you to drink."

"Don't drive while you're drinking."

"When can we expect *Leave Her to Heaven*?"

"Can I call it that?"

"Titles can't be copyrighted."

Mr. Victor had been the school librarian at Toledo high, a timid man with defective hearing, an object of mockery by students. This drew Rosa to him. He seemed happy to have one student who was polite and deferential. Five years ago he had moved to the public library in a western suburb. He had guessed that she was the author of the glossy paperbacks that began to appear around Toledo.

"How did you guess?"

"*The Grapes of Wrath*."

That had been her favorite Steinbeck. Remembering how the novel ended, with Rose of Sharon nursing the starving man, Rosa blushed, but Mr. Victor gave no indication that he remembered the scene. Regularly he sent her little notes of congratulation, including a notice of her new book in *Library Journal* or *Publishers Weekly*. He was actually proud of her. And he began his campaign to get her to speak at his library.

"I never give speeches."

"Just talk about your work."

It was an aspect of being a successful author that she had denied herself. Sometimes it seemed that writers spent more time promoting a book than they had writing it. If it were anyone other than Mr. Victor, she would have squashed the invitation once and for all.

One of the disconcerting things about Julius Sweeney was his resemblance to Mr. Victor. Of course he had been much younger, but it bothered Rosa that somehow subconsciously she had been avenging herself on the one man who had accepted her as a person. She had gotten three novels out of that

thought, variations on the theme of each man—or woman—
kills the thing he loves. That was the kind of tragic plot that
was sure-fire with Rosa's readers. A heroine reaching for the
stars but always fated to fall to earth, spent and rejected. A
new editor had urged Rosa to write a story with a happy
ending but she knew enough about herself to recognize the
source of her inspiration.

"No endings are happy."

"You can't believe that."

"It's not a matter of belief."

Franklin had the editor yanked as if to prove what Rosa
had told her.

"What kind of setting would it be?" Rosa asked Mr. Victor
when she began to weaken. She still thought of him as Mr.
Victor even after she learned that was his first name. Victor
Armitage. She told him he had been using a pseudonym all
these years.

"You should talk."

"All nyms are pseudo." But it came out nymphs, the slip of
the tongue an occupational hazard of the romance novelist.

Rosa agreed to speak at the Toledo public library. Victor
acted as if he had scored a real coup. When the publicity
began—print, radio, a brochure available to library patrons—
Rosa began to panic. The photograph Victor used had been
supplied by her publisher, and it was the only photograph
Rosa's readers had ever seen, it appeared on all of her novels
ascribed to Rosa Charrin. For other pseudonyms, the publisher morphed file photos of mindlessly beautiful women
who did not look as if they had the attention span to write a
paragraph, let alone a novel.

She drove over to Toledo early one morning to see what
the setting for the talk would be. It was the podium that al-

layed her fears. She would speak from behind that, standing on a stool that would make her look average height. She would affect a floppy brimmed hat and large glasses. If she spoke with her hands, she could divert attention from her face. Her voice came through marvelously.

"The voice of an actress," Victor said.

"Fittingly enough."

But as the date approached, Rosa became increasingly nervous and found it difficult to write even five thousand words a day. She cursed herself for agreeing to Victor's insistent demands. She had a dream in which she took him to bed and then threw him into the Prune from a high bridge. She had nothing but a cup of yogurt and nine cups of coffee before she set off for Toledo to give her talk on "The Open Secrets of Writing Success."

7

Fred Huff learned shorthand in order to get a job as a court reporter but by the time he applied they were using machines. He tried to get the hang of it, he thought of going back to school and learning the process slowly, but the part-time job at the fast food place quickly evolved into a managerial position. He might have lived his life supervising the cooking of hamburgers and frying of potatoes if he hadn't met Edna at a place where he went to play bridge.

"It's only temporary," he said when he saw the way she reacted.

"What's permanent going to be?"

"Real estate."

Later he would ask himself where that answer had come from. There were magazines of local real estate in racks at the door of the fast food place, and he had probably overheard salesmen talking, but he had never dreamed of selling real estate. He wasn't sure he could sell anything. Edna was impressed, however; she seemed to know that a very good income indeed was possible in real estate. So he took a course and landed the job at Thompson's in Toledo.

At the fast food job he had occupied a position of responsibility and authority. The turnover was terrific, kids replacing kids, endlessly, and as far as they knew he had been Mr. Kroch's partner when he opened the first restaurant. At

Thompson's he was on the lowest rung of a crowded ladder. All around him in the office were agents who routinely sold a million dollars worth of housing a year, sometimes multiples of that. They were the kind of real estate agent Edna must have heard of. Fred did not like to think what their income was, compared to his.

"I have to hold you to the minimum level of sales, Fred," Thompson told him, in one of the talks they had during Fred's first year. "You were chosen from a rather large application pool."

Why? What had Thompson seen or thought he saw in Fred's application? Edna had helped him with it, and it was a bitter thought that he was employed on a misunderstanding. Thompson thought he was hiring Edna. It was one more item to add to his growing litany of grievances against her.

Even more mysterious than what Thompson had seen in him, was what Edna had seen in him. She often asked herself that question, aloud, as she walked away from him. He had disappointed her. At Thompson's he unfailingly hit the minimum amount of sales and kept his job, a job he hated. He could not bear to stop at the fast food place and feel the rush of happy memories. He would never have left if it hadn't been for Edna pushing him. It was that same doggedness that kept him tied to a wife he did not love, largely because she held him in such obvious contempt. He dreamt of leaving her the same way he dreamt of leaving Thompson's and going back into fast food. He wasn't much, but for a time at least he had been enough for Edna, a meal ticket, however meager, that freed her to play duplicate bridge three days a week. The other days she played bingo. But it was her treatment of their more or less relatives that had killed any remaining affection he had for her, not least because she implicated him in the way she treated them.

When Vivian Yates was dying he would have liked to go to the hospital and tell her how good she had been to take in her father-in-law even though he had Alzheimer's. Sometimes he thought it was the old man's disability that had been the deciding factor. If the old man had been able to live alone she would have let him do it, who wants to move into someone else's house? Of course he never did tell her. Somehow Edna would have heard of it and then his life would have become even worse. When she told him, after Vivian died, that they were moving to Fort Elbow, he resisted.

"I work in Toledo."

She thought about it, then nodded. "Yes, you should go on working."

"You wouldn't have wanted to take care of the old man," he said, magnanimous in what he thought was victory.

"I meant that you can commute."

Fred just stared at her, unable to believe that she would expect him to make that long drive back and forth every day. "I'll quit first."

"You will not."

It was the sweetest defeat he ever suffered. The long commute and then all day in Toledo gave him a freedom he had not had since he married her. He could come home late and blame it on the traffic and she never questioned him about it. He would fix his own supper and eat it alone in the kitchen, with Edna commandeering the television in the living room. Soon it would be time to go to bed. The house gave them separate bedrooms and why not? Edna's fear of pregnancy had put him on slim rations in that department from the beginning and they had long since drifted away from intimacy. He took pleasure in the thought that he was asleep most of the time he was under the same roof as his wife.

Now he had a powerful motive to meet the minimum

quota in sales as quickly as he could, the better to have his day to himself. Even so he was careful. He watched a lot of movies, going to West Toledo and the mall theater there, lest he be seen by one of Edna's old bridge friends who might mention it to Edna. The fast food places in the mall did not stir up old regrets. It was in the fish place that he met Hazel.

"How long have you been a widower, Fred?"

"Oh, I still think of myself as married."

Hazel was manager of the restaurant and with her he could speak of his own time in the fast food community.

"You were smart to get out."

"I wish I hadn't."

"You're kidding." Hazel knew he was in real estate and imagined he was a hotshot salesman. Whenever he dropped by to see her, he said he was in West Toledo to show a multiple listing. When he learned her schedule, he knew what days he could suggest she come to a movie with him.

"I want to celebrate a sale."

"What do you make on a house?"

"This was an apartment building." He told her what percentage the agent makes. "Of course it's less on a multiple listing." He could see her doing rapid calculations in her head. She must think he was swimming in money.

"You aren't listed in the Toledo phone directory."

"I live in Fort Elbow."

"Fort Elbow!"

"It's a far more interesting town." And he could see that she was imagining the impossibly interesting life he led in the largest city in the area.

In the theater, they shared a box of popcorn and when their hands kept meeting among the kernels he realized it was not by accident. They held hands after the popcorn was gone, although her hand was greasy with butter and Fred had become impossibly neat after years with Edna. He felt he was having the kind of time he had not had before he married.

Hazel had been married twice. Two strikes, as she called it. No children, thank God, though God knew she had tried. But her first husband drank and was seldom up to the task and her second turned out to be sterile after he was tested when all their amorous labors proved in vain.

"It begins to lose its meaning when there's no prospect of children."

"Do you still hope for them?"

She said she was in her mid-thirties, but Fred guessed her to be at least forty. Even so it was not biologically impossible. Was she sizing him up as a stud? She certainly was not niggardly in her affections. She said she wanted to cook for him but he said he had to go back to Fort Elbow every night.

"But why?"

He hesitated and then told her he was the guardian of both his niece and of his wife's father. "He has Alzheimer's."

She looked at him with the kind of admiration he had felt for Vivian.

"I'll have to have you for lunch." And her eyes widened significantly as she said it.

It became what was called an affair, and it seemed as improbable to Fred as it would have to Edna. She would never suspect him of spending his days in Toledo as he did, let alone that he might have someone like Hazel in love with him.

"I could never marry again," he told Hazel.

"Good. Marriage would only spoil what we have."

They were like kids together at first, soaping one another in the shower, watching videos Hazel had bought, mattress instructions for lovers. But passion cooled after a time, as passion will, and while there were still luxuriant afternoon hours in her bed, they became friends as well. How he wished he could tell her the truth about himself. How he wished he had the nerve to leave Edna and convince Hazel that marriage would only solidify their relationship. He told himself he could not abandon Lucy and Grandpa Yates to the domination of Edna.

He managed the household accounts and made sure that Lucy always had plenty of money.

"Uncle Fred, I don't need it."

"It's yours."

"But you need it to pay the bills."

She really seemed unaware of how much money she had put them in charge of.

The day Hazel told him of the blind man who had been missing for weeks and then showed up wandering around the parking lot of the mall, Fred felt a sudden chill. One of Lucy's fears was that Grandpa would get lost and be unable to tell anyone who he was.

"Sew his name in his clothes."

"I did. But they keep coming off in the wash."

The one thing that Edna did in return for the money they were taking from Lucy was the laundry.

When he saw the notice of the writer who had been born in Toledo and was returning to speak at the library, Fred peered at the picture, certain he had seen that face before. It came to him when he was at the movies with Hazel. She squeezed his hand hard, and he realized that he had squeezed hers when he realized that Rosa Charrin had once worked at Thompson's, an ugly but efficient girl they had hidden in a back room lest she frighten away clients. Imagine her being a writer! He had half a mind to make an excuse to stay late and go hear her.

8

Nick Byers was working his way through college by editing the giveaway newspaper published by the mall in Toledo. He only went down there a couple times a week, to gather material for the stories he would write, but he could write anywhere. The job gave him the illusion that he was Hemingway working on the *Kansas City Star*, serving a necessary apprenticeship for his career as an author. Of course Hemingway had never gone to college, he certainly had never taken courses in creative writing.

Nick despised himself for despising Miss McManus. His contempt was for himself, sitting through those classes seemingly meant to turn everyone into a writer of unreadable stories that were painfully autobiographical. Even though Miss McManus went on about Aristotle and the need for plot, the student stories she gushed over had less development than a Chekov sketch. Nick wanted to be a writer in the mold of Hemingway and Roth and Updike, guys who had made a good living from their fiction but who were the best there was as well. Writing for the mall paper was almost as embarrassing as taking creative writing. Lucy got all excited when he told her about editing *Flourishes*.

"Why *Flourishes*?"

He winced. "It's what you do with a cape."

"So?"

"Bullfighting. Toledo, Spain. Look, it wasn't my choice."

But the rough idea had been his and he had convinced Hutchinson, the mall manager, to give him a six-month trial. He made sure the manager was mentioned several times in every issue and his job was secure. He didn't tell Lucy that his preferred name for the paper was *Veronica*. Hutchinson had just looked at him blankly and Nick explained it to him.

"People will think it's a woman." Actually that was the name of a girl Nick had hoped to go with at the time.

Hutchinson proposed *Flourishes*. "It captures the same idea, and it's far less confusing."

Whenever Nick wrote something he thought was particularly good, he tried to sell it to the local paper. He would have given it away for a chance to appear in print in a real newspaper, but no one respects a writer who writes for nothing. He hung around the water fountain that was the centerpiece of the mall, observing the old people, listening. It seemed sad that a life should end like this. These people had led real lives, held interesting jobs, raised children and done lots of things, and now they sat in their gym shoes and stared at a phony fountain. Even the water looked phony. The story he wrote had a good balance of sentiment and detachment. The local paper did not want it. When Hutchinson read it, he was impressed.

"Better brighten it up, though."

"How so."

"You make this seem a place where people are waiting to die."

Lucy's eyes filled with tears when she read it and afterward she gave him a kiss, the ultimate seal of her approval.

"It is so sad, Nick. It makes me think of Grandpa."

Nick thought of Lucy's grandfather when the missing blind man was found in the mall over in West Toledo. He went over there to find out more and was surprised to run into Lucy's uncle.

"I was showing a house," Fred said, his manner jumpy.

He was in a fast food place that specialized in fish. Nick talked to the manager who seemed to know all about the blind man.

"How do you know Fred?"

"I date his niece."

"It's a small world."

Fred seemed to think it was too small. Nick wrote up the story of the blind man, certain that this time he had a winner, but it was nixed without explanation. He couldn't run it in *Flourishes* and he didn't want to show it to Lucy, fearful it would sadden her. He made up a story to tell her if Uncle Fred mentioned seeing him in West Toledo, but apparently he never did.

Nick knew about Rosa Charrin. Every female relative of his read Rosa Charrin. Given her output, Nick suggested that there was a platoon of writers turning out Rosa Charrin stories and was nearly run out of the house. Nick had read his share of her novels, though he would never admit it. He infinitely preferred her prolific output and wide readership to the ideal of the author Miss McManus seemed to promote. Rosa was a craftsman. Nick wondered if she had read Aristotle. Naw. She was a phenomenon, a natural. There were worse things than being a hack writer, things like being either unpublished or unread. He had been half kidding when he suggested to Lucy that they go hear the writer speak at the public library in Toledo. He would have gone alone and he was almost disappointed when Lucy agreed. Rosa was certainly no Willa Cather.

"I saw your uncle the other day," he told her, wondering what her reaction would be.

"Poor Uncle Fred, driving back and forth to Toledo every day."

They were on the highway, on their way to hear Rosa speak. Rain was falling and every once in a while there was a flash of lightning across the lowering sky. Lucy sat close beside Nick, hugging his arm.

"This weather might keep people away."

But the library auditorium was almost full when they got there, row after row of excitedly whispering fans, about to see in the flesh the writer in whose fantasies they took half-ashamed pleasure. She and the manager took places at the table in front while Nick and Lucy were finding seats in the back row. The writer looked mysterious in glasses and a huge hat and stared at Victor Armitage, the director, while he went through a long and unctuous introduction, telling the audience things they knew as well as he did. And then he was escorting the writer to the podium and she loomed above them.

"The first thing you should know is that no writer should be believed when he tells you about himself. Or herself, for that matter. After all, fiction is a form of lying."

The lying that was done in the novels of Rosa Charrin was largely horizontal, but it was a good beginning. The people had come on a rainy night prepared to love her and she spoke with such confident authority of her craft that Lucy too sat forward in rapt attention.

Afterward, there was a crush around the podium as the audience pressed forward with books to sign. There were copies of some of her novels on sale, which surprised Nick. In a library? Rosa remained at the podium as she signed the books and after twenty minutes Nick and Lucy gave up all hope of talking to her.

"I want to write this up," Nick said. "I wish I could interview her."

"Telephone her."

"Good idea."

Or so it seemed until he failed to find a listing for her in any of the area phone books. He tried information.

"That's an unlisted number."

"But I'm a journalist."

"I'm sorry."

"Oh, it's not as bad a job as all that."

9

The plan had been forming in her mind for weeks and when Fred said he would be staying in Toledo later than usual, and Lucy too would be there to hear a writer lecture, Edna knew that the moment had come. Suddenly it seemed that she could not stand another day in the house with Grandpa Yates.

Of late he had developed the annoying habit of making a mewling noise as he sat in his chair, looking at the television as if he could not see it or did not know what it was, his hands gripping the arms of the chair. What a useless thing he was. His life was over, he had died inside, and yet he sat there as if he were attending his own wake, making that aggravating sound.

It did no good to tell him to shut up, although sometimes Edna was convinced he understood and went on moaning in order to annoy her. People professed to be shocked by Doctor Kevorkian, but Edna thought the man had the right idea. Imagine if Vivian had lingered on in unendurable pain. Was it really different with Grandpa?

Not that she planned to do anything drastic. She had come to see her plan as similar to buying a ticket in the lottery. She would do what she planned to do and either it would work or it would not. If it did not, no one would know what she had done and Grandpa could certainly not tell on her.

She had already looked into car rentals and as soon as

49

Lucy left with Nick, Edna made the call. But when she took Grandpa's hand to lead him to her own car, he refused to move. Edna had often struck him when she was alone with the idiot and now, angered at this delay in executing her plan, she slapped him very hard across the face. That did it. She took his hand and pulled him through the house and into the garage. He jumped in fright as the garage doors went up, but she got him into the passenger seat and slammed the door on him.

The plan was that she would drive to the airport, pick up the rental car, transfer Grandpa to it, and then she would be truly under way. She did not realize how heavily it was raining until she backed out of the garage and the thundering on the roof began.

"Shut up," she cried, when Grandpa began to whine.

He cowered in a corner of the seat. Edna straightened him up and got the seat belt on him. He was terrified of her now. Good.

She was halfway to the airport when she noticed the warning light come on. The needle of the gas gauge stood at empty. She should stop for gas, that was the sensible thing, but she did not want to be seen with the old man in the car beside her tonight, not if her gamble paid off. She drove slowly, hoping to conserve gas and she ran a stop light rather than sit waiting for it to change with the motor burning gas all the while. When finally she turned in at the airport and saw the ugly terminal illumined before her, she waived all her misgivings about its style and found it a loveable object.

The motor died just as she entered short term parking and had punched the button to get her ticket. Of all places, she could not just leave her car here. And if she went for help, Grandpa would be seen and she would have to scrap the whole idea and come up with something else. Holding her breath, eyes shut, she twisted the ignition key off then on, and the motor sputtered into life. She entered the lot with momentum and pulled into a parking place as the motor died finally.

"Wait here," she said to Grandpa, which was stupid, he wouldn't know what she meant. But he nodded.

"You understand?"

He nodded. Lucy had told her that there were fleeting moments when his mind seemed to clear. This must be one of them. Edna got out of the car, eased the door shut and then walked rapidly toward the terminal.

"Lucy Yates," she said to the girl behind the counter.

"Driver's license."

She had anticipated that question, fortunately, and filched Lucy's license from her purse a week ago when the plan had finally firmed in her mind. Lucy had discovered the absence of the license and had applied for another and was now equipped with a temporary permit. The girl just glanced at the license, saw that it was valid, and pushed it back across the counter. Even if she had looked, the photographs on driving licenses were notoriously bad. Minutes later, having signed and initialed the form, Edna was given the keys plus instructions on where she would find the car.

Outside the terminal doors, she stood for a moment and took a deep breath. Her original plan had been to get the rental car, drive back to the terminal, park in the street and fetch Grandpa from the car. Now it seemed more sensible to take him with her to the car. She crossed the street as the canned announcement came over the loudspeaker warning drivers who parked in No Parking zones that their cars would be ticketed and towed. Ticketed and towed. Edna chanted the phrase aloud as she crossed to the parking lot. Grandpa was not in the car.

Edna pulled the door open and stared at the empty passenger seat, astounded, while thoughts roared through her mind like a freight train. Was this how it was meant to happen? But how could she explain driving to the airport and the rental car would become known and . . . No.

Edna slammed the door shut and looked around at the silent cars in the lot. And then she saw him, standing between two cars looking vacantly around. He did not seem alarmed. Edna was too relieved to be angry with him. She took his hand and led him across the lot in the direction of the rental cars. Suddenly the whole place seemed deserted, as if she and Grandpa were the only ones there. After the scare at not finding him in the car, Edna now felt that her plan was bound to succeed.

She did not bother buckling Grandpa up when she settled him in the passenger seat of the rental car, but when he pitched forward the first time she applied the brakes, she pulled over and pulled the strap across his chest, and snapped it tight.

"There," she said.

"Thank you."

"You're welcome."

It was the most conversation she had ever had with him, if that is what it was. As she drove, she told him what she was going to do, and why. It was for Lucy's sake. If he had half a mind he would understand and agree, but of course if he had even half a mind things wouldn't have come to this.

"I never liked you," she told him.

He had been staring straight ahead but conscious of her eyes on him he turned. Suddenly he gave her a radiant smile.

Edna stopped talking and kept her eyes on the road.

She was taking him to West Toledo, for luck. He would be found wandering around in the parking lot and when they asked him who he was he wouldn't know. Edna had removed all the nametags that Lucy insisted on sewing into his clothes. His pockets were empty, she had removed his watch—what does an idiot need with a watch? Besides, it might help identify him. He would be a confused old man who did not know his own name and who had nothing on him that could possibly identify him. Edna was relying on the mall to keep publicity to a minimum. It would begin to look like an epidemic, lost old men wandering around their parking lot. It was unlikely to make the Fort Elbow paper, but if it did Edna would intercept it and keep the story from Lucy. Fred? Edna made a snorting sound. She would take care of Fred.

With Grandpa gone, becoming an anonymous public ward, the house would be more normal. Soon Lucy would graduate and find a teaching job, almost certainly not in Fort Elbow. The time of aggravation would be past. Finally the house would be Edna's.

It was odd how she had to remind herself that she still had Fred.

The parking lot of the West Toledo mall was vast. There were many cars in one area, near the movie theater, but by and large it had thinned out considerably at this hour. But there were still late shoppers and of course the clerks would be leaving after ten.

Someone would be sure to find Grandpa and call the police.

When she stopped and put the car in Park she did not turn off the motor. She undid Grandpa's seat belt and leaned across him to open the door. He put his arms around her and began to rock her gently.

"Stop that!"

He stopped and his arms dropped. Honestly. She got the door open.

"Get out."

53

He did not hesitate. Like a domesticated animal he responded to certain basic commands. Outside, he stood beside the car, waiting.

"Shut the door."

He shut the door. Edna looked around to see if they were observed, and was certain they were not. Her lights had been extinguished. She put the car in Drive and the car pulled slowly away from Grandpa. She could see him in the rearview mirror, just standing there. Almost, she felt sorry for him.

Part Two

TWITCH

1

Victor called to tell Rosa that the young reporter would not let go of the idea of interviewing her. He himself highly recommended the young fellow.

"He wants to be a writer."

"He already is a writer if he's a reporter."

"You know what I mean."

"He should have talked to me that night."

"I explained all that. He couldn't get near you."

The talk had gone as well as Victor predicted it would. For the course of an evening she had been what people thought she was, a successful writer, at ease with her success, perhaps living a life as fulfilling as one of her heroine's. Could she continue to play the role of successful author? A whole new vista opened before her, one that canceled out the dark moments of her past. Someone at the library had asked her if she thought there could be a perfect crime.

"For the victim?" Everything she said was greeted as witty or profound. "Oh, from the criminal's point of view. Of course. I have done many dreadful things and been undetected. Haven't you?"

"But you never murdered anyone?"

"Not lately."

Playing with fire. She had found it exhilarating. And it could become addictive. That is why she was determined

57

there would be no sequel to her successful talk. She had ful-
filled an obligation to Victor and that was all it was. She
would far rather write than talk about it.

So she was settled down again in her cork lined room and
had begun a new novel, planning for it to be twice as large as
anything she had yet written. How wonderful it was to sit before her word processor and enter the world of imagination
where she herself was surprised at the images and plot com-
plications that came unbidden.

"He edits the mall newspaper," Victor said of the impor-
tuning journalist.

"That makes him a reporter?"

"He would write it for the local paper."

The mention of the mall intrigued her. And no wonder.
Sometimes she wished that she had kept Julius, someone in
whom she could confide, companionship. And her wish had
been granted.

After the talk, before leaving West Toledo, she drove to
the mall where she had set Julius free. She had parked and sat
in her darkened car and felt the world close in on her. While
she sat there, a car went slowly past and then came slowly
back again. Rosa wondered if she was going to be the
unwilling secret sharer of some quick lovemaking in the
parking lot. The woman behind the wheel lunged at her passenger and they embraced, but then the door opened. The
man who got out was not agile. He shut the door and stood
there and then the car pulled away. A hundred yards from
the man, the lights were turned on and then the car went out
of sight.

Rosa had waited, fascinated, sure the woman would come
back for the man. But he continued to stand there. Rosa
started her engine and then driving without lights, as the
woman had, she moved slowly toward the standing man. She

pulled up beside him and opened the door.

"Get in."

To her amazement he did. She was disappointed to find that he was an old man. Her successful lecture had filled her with what her characters would think of as the fleshly desires, but her ancient passenger promised no relief from them.

Never had she had such a docile companion. He was quiet, well-mannered, perpetually confused, but any special wariness he felt at being brought home by her soon vanished. She did not stow him in the basement as she had Julius, but gave him the bedroom which, for a short time, had served as her writing room, before she had her present study remodeled to her specifications. After a couple of novels, she had a better sense of the working conditions that were best for her. She had put him to bed and he slept like a baby.

There was no cry of alarm in the next day's papers, frantic family desperately seeking lost senior. He perked up when she called him Grandpa and that became her name for him. While he slept, she had searched his clothes for some clue as to who he was, but the clothes were as anonymous as he was. Even the brand name labels had been removed. Ripped out, in some cases.

The only item at all was the lottery ticket, a Power Ball bought some days before.

The next day, before she could feed him breakfast—raisin bran with skim milk with a glass of juice on the side—he looked at her in confusion and rubbed his chin. She soaped up his face right there, draping a towel over his shoulders, and using her own razor shaved him. What fine unwrinkled skin he had. She found that she was talking to him constantly. Alone, she had formed the habit of talking aloud to herself, why not. The habit had gone into abeyance when Julius was with her, but Grandpa was so silent, the whole burden of sociability was up to her.

"She dumped you, Grandpa. She drove you to that mall and left you there. You're lucky I saw it."

A medium sized, silver white sedan, probably a Toyota, Ohio plates. The old man wasn't a barrel of laughs but neither was he a problem. After finishing his cereal and juice, he took his things to the sink and rinsed them out. He stood still then, looking at the coffeepot. Well, she could start in on her daily consumption now. She tried to put it off until midmorning, since once she started drinking coffee it was nonstop until sundown, cup after cup.

Grandpa would have stood there by the sink all day if she had not led him back to his chair, assuring him that coffee was on its way. He wasn't retarded, that wasn't it; it had to be Alzheimer's. Rosa decided it would be better if she thought of him as ignorant of English and as they sat over their coffee, she tried fragments of languages on him. But he was no more responsive than he was to English. The question was, what was he going to do all day?

The answer was, sit quietly in her study while she wrote. He was neither interested nor disinterested in what she did, or in what happened to him. The problem crept into Rosa's story and that became a way of trying to figure out what had happened in the mall, and why, and what his background was.

But why a lottery ticket? Was that the equivalent of money in the thumb of a mitten, or mad money in a woman's purse? The lottery ticket fascinated her the most, but she could not fit that into her novel, given the setting of the story in the ante-bellum South.

There was nothing on the radio news about a lost old man and nothing later on television.

"That's it, Grandpa. You're an abandoned baby."

"Lucy," he said suddenly, speech coming from him like a biblical miracle. Just that, a name, and then he resumed his placid silence.

Lucy. A name, a Toyota with an Ohio license, a lottery ticket, and a woman seen indistinctly as she drove away from Grandpa. How could she have done that to such a nice old man? He was no trouble at all. When he got up and began to wander around, it occurred to her that he was looking for the bathroom, so she showed him where it was. Twenty minutes later, he was still in there. Rosa eased open the door to find him standing there, waiting for her. Was he done? Did he need help? But he stepped out of the bathroom and went back down the hallway to the study and sat once more in the chair she had put him in before. That answered that.

Rosa did not eat lunch, but she made a toasted cheese sandwich for Grandpa and he ate it along with soda.

"What did you do for a living?"

She might have been speaking to the refrigerator. But his silence was almost restful, and he was a good companion for her, a spur to her writing, if anything. She would have thought that a silent witness in the corner would have stopped her cold, but Grandpa was like a lucky charm. The first day he was with her she wrote seven thousand words, not bad.

"Maybe we'll win the lottery."

"Lucy."

2

It had been nearly midnight when they got back to Fort Elbow, it was nearly midnight but the conversation on the highway had been so interesting that they stopped at an all-night restaurant and continued talking until after one. By the time Nick dropped her off, it was as late as Lucy had ever come home since Edna and Fred had moved in with her and she half expected her aunt to be standing in the doorway, tapping her foot. But the house was silent. Lucy tiptoed to her room, not even looking in on Grandpa, and fell almost immediately asleep.

"Lucy!"

Her aunt's cry lifted her from the bed more surely than any alarm clock could have. Edna stood in the doorway, in her dressing gown, her hair actually mussed, a wild look in her eyes. Lucy's first thought was that something had happened to Fred.

"What is it?"

"Grandpa's gone! He's not in his room."

Lucy jumped from her bed and ran down the hallway to his room. Not only was it empty, the bed was still made. She felt a mad impulse to blame Edna, but guilt flooded through her when she thought of being away until the early hours. It was now seven. If only she had looked into this room last night.

"When did you last see him?"

Edna crossed her arms. "You're certainly calm about it."

"Did you see him last night?"

"We watched television together but he went to his room at the usual time."

"Nine o'clock."

"Maybe earlier."

Lucy would have bet on earlier. She could believe that Edna just locked Grandpa in his room to stare at the walls, all alone. A single sob burst forth from Lucy, but then she was on her feet.

"I'm going to look for him."

"Look for him!"

"Edna, how far could he have gone?"

In the dark. It wrenched Lucy's heart to think of Grandpa confused and alone and outside at nighttime. She dressed hurriedly and checked the house, to make sure he wasn't just seated somewhere, perhaps to get away from Edna.

She searched the yard and the garage without result. She went into the kitchen where Edna was seated at the table, staring.

"Where's Fred?"

"He left before I realized . . ."

"Could he have . . ." It was a mad thought, Fred taking Grandpa to work with him, all the way to Toledo, as a treat for the old man. Fat chance.

Chance! She thought of the lottery ticket she had put into the breast pocket of the corduroy sport jacket he always wore, their little secret. She had written down the numbers after she had decided that tearing the ticket in two and giving him one half and keeping the other might make it invalid. It was their secret little investment, and she had assured Grandpa that they would win. How sweetly he had followed her explanation, not understanding anything.

"Edna, don't call the police."

"The police!"

"I am going to take my car and search the neighborhood. He can't have gone far."

How had he spent the night? She imagined him lying, shivering and terrified on someone's lawn, under a tree, perhaps on a patio. Anyone who found a confused old man sleeping on their porch would immediately call the police. No, the neighbors knew about Grandpa and would have called Lucy.

The car wasn't a good idea, since she had to get out to look about in people's yards. In the second one, a door opened and a man she didn't recognize glared at her.

"Can I help you?"

"Have you seen an old man?"

The weirdness of the question all but overwhelmed her. She launched into a long explanation, mentioning the Alzheimer's, and the man's manner changed. He came outside and looked around his yard, even into the garage and a small tool shed set back in a far corner of the lot.

"How long has he been missing?"

"His bed wasn't slept in."

"Has he done this before?"

"Never."

"Look, someone is bound to notice him and call the police."

When Lucy first thought of the police, and told Edna not to call them, she had been thinking of how awful it sounded, losing Grandpa, but that was silly. She got back in her car and drove home. Edna was still sitting at the kitchen table, like Grandpa did, just staring. Lucy went to the phone and dialed 911.

"I want to report a missing man who has Alzheimer's."

Edna lifted from her chair as she heard the message and

Lucy could see that her aunt was thinking as she had earlier. Her mouth opened as if to protest, but then closed. She sat down, picked up her cup and stared into it, as if she were reading tea leaves.

The police had no report of an old man with Alzheimer's.

"You should come down and make out a report."

It was something to do, at least, and it seemed the only thing as well. The man who had said that someone was bound to find Grandpa and call the police was surely right. On the way to the precinct station, she had an impulse to call Nick, he could be of help to her in a way no one else could, but she didn't. She was almost surprised at how firmly Nick seemed to have established himself in her life.

There was something almost reassuring about the missing person form she was asked to fill out. It reduced the loss of Grandpa to the ordinary. Why would you print up special forms if people were not missing all the time? The cop who handed it to her was a woman, in a uniform that brought out all the bulges in the worst way; she seemed to be impersonating a man. Her plastic name badge read Jo Kuss. Lucy tried to imagine her in a dress. Would she still swagger when she walked, her keys and cuffs and pistol rolling with the rhythm of her hips? But she was helpful and expressed genuine sympathy when she realized what had happened.

"My dad lives with us."

Lucy nodded, as if they were members of a secret society.

"Half the time I wish he would take a walk."

"What does your husband say?"

"He already took a walk. No, I ran him off."

It was another world, here at the police station. Lucy tried to imagine Grandpa sitting here, waiting. He was always waiting.

In her car, she rested her forehead against the wheel and whispered to her mother to help Grandpa be found.

"I'm sorry," she found herself saying, over and over. "I'm so sorry."

And then she thought of Alex and started the car.

3

"Good," Alex said when Lucy said she had filed a missing persons report with the police. "They'll find him."

No point in feeding her anxiety, and guilt. She was blaming herself for what had happened. How like her mother she was. Vivian had felt guilty about how comfortable she had been left as a widow and the only way he had been able to assuage her guilt was to work out arrangements whereby it was gradually transferred into Lucy's name. When Vivian died that had saved an awful lot on inheritance taxes. Of course Alex did not mention such mundane legal facts to Lucy.

Lucy gave no indication that she suspected her aunt and uncle in the matter, but Alex could easily imagine Edna leaving the door open and suggesting to Grandpa that he go outside. The old man had several times become lost in the back yard, having forgotten the house in which he lived, though it was right there before his eyes. Of course, Grandpa had not become lost. Being lost was his permanent condition. In his heart of hearts, Alex shared the impatience of Edna with the old man, though her impatience was greedy. When at last Grandpa went to his reward, there would be fewer cuts in the pie. Thank God Edna had no idea of how well off her niece really was.

"Will you urge the police, Alex?"

"Of course. Don't worry. Uncle Alex will do whatever can be done."

That turned out not to be much. No report of a man answering to Grandpa's description had been reported.

"He can't have just disappeared."

Detective Noonan took his unlit cigar from his mouth and studied it before looking up at Alex. "Most likely now, given the time he's been gone, something's happened to him."

The image of the old man lying dead in a ditch made Alex feel sick.

"Of course he might have been kidnapped."

"What for?"

Noonan shrugged and returned his cigar to the corner of his mouth. He had quit smoking cigarettes for health reasons and now seemed determined to get cancer of the mouth.

Improbable as kidnapping seemed, it was preferable to thinking of the old man lying dead somewhere. Alex had read of raccoons, or was it coyotes, ravaging derelicts. He thought of the crows that descended on road kill, risking their own death to tug away at carrion. What would they care what species the body was? Back in his car, out of sight of Noonan, he permitted himself to shiver. No, he preferred the unlikely possibility that Grandpa had been kidnapped.

Not that Noonan had suggested it seriously. Kidnappers wanted something and they got in contact with the one who could give it to them. Lucy was willing enough to come to his office and Alex did not want to talk about the matter in front of Edna.

"How is your aunt taking it?"

"She's frantic of course. She has bought half a dozen papers, certain some story of Grandpa has been written."

"He has to be found first."

"There would have been no way to identify him."

68

"All the more reason we would have heard. But you mean that, there was no identification on him? In his pockets . . ."

"The name tags I sewed on his clothes came off in the wash. Maybe he took them off."

"Why would he do that?"

"Just to be doing something, I don't know."

He gave her a moment to settle down. The strain was beginning to tell on Lucy. "The police mentioned, just as a possibility, kidnapping, but that makes no sense in his case."

"I wish he had been!"

"Kidnapped?"

"Yes. Then he would be somewhere, safe, inside, and we would hear."

That made a kind of sense, Alex supposed.

"If only I hadn't gone to Toledo that night."

"Tell me about it."

But she couldn't stay with the talk at the public library, her mind darted back to what Grandpa was doing while she sat there listening to an author talk of the books she had written.

"I got home late and didn't check his room. If I had, if I had started looking for him right away . . ."

"Edna and Fred were home?"

"Yes."

After Lucy left, Alex called Fred at Thompson's in Toledo and they got in contact with him on his beeper. He called Alex an hour later.

"I want to talk to you about what happened to Grandpa."

"Do you know, I left the house this morning not realizing that . . . The poor old guy."

"Where can we meet?"

"I suppose you could come to the house tonight."

"Could you come here?"

69

"I'm with a client, Alex."

"In Toledo?"

"West Toledo."

"I could meet you there."

They met at the mall and Fred suggested they use one of the conference rooms at Kinko's. Fred was a different man away from Edna and Alex wondered if this was the man he had learned to despise for the way he let his wife trample on him.

"Tell me about last night."

"When Grandpa apparently left the house?"

"When did you last see him that night?"

"Oh, I wasn't home."

"You weren't."

"A former employee of ours was speaking at the library here and I stayed over to hear her."

"Is that the woman Lucy went to hear?"

"I thought I saw Lucy there."

"Did she see you?"

"She hasn't mentioned it. Of course we have been caught up in what happened to Grandpa."

"So Edna was home alone with Grandpa that night?"

"Yes."

Just yes, then silence, and it grew to be an almost accusation. "He must be a trial for you."

"For me?"

"You and Edna."

"I like him, I always have. Look, Edna is Edna, she doesn't show her real feelings . . ."

He stopped as if he were failing to convince himself. But what he said meant that Edna had treated Grandpa badly, but of course Alex already knew that.

"Lucy says he had no identification on him."

"For Lucy's sake, I wish this would be cleared up. Even if the worst has happened, it is better than not knowing."

"The worst has happened to Lucy too often."

"Would you include me and Edna in that?"

"I meant her parents and now this."

"I didn't want to move from Toledo."

It suddenly hit Alex what that move had meant for Fred, a long commute every day, while Edna settled into Fort Elbow. But Fred looked content enough, there in the conference room at Kinko's. And he talked about what had happened in Fort Elbow as if it did not really involve him.

"What was the name of that author you heard speak?"

"Rosa Charrin. Ever hear of her?"

"What does she write?"

"Love stories. When she worked for us you would have said she was doomed to be a flop in life. She was good at her job, very good, and she might have gone on doing that, making that her life."

"Not all that fulfilling."

Fred grew thoughtful. "Who's to say? I'm married and you're not. Are we models of what life is all about? Anyway she has struck it big and I'm glad for her."

"Have you read any of her stuff?"

"I bought one that night and got her to autograph it."

"What was her name again?"

"Rosa Subiaco was the name I knew her by."

"Did she change it?"

"She writes under pen names."

4

"Why don't you just write a story on what I said at the library?"

"Of course I'll include that," Nick said. He had given Victor Armitage his phone number, urging him to pass it along to Rosa when it was clear he was not going to get her number. Now to his surprise, the author had called. Victor had already told her of Nick's hope to do a feature on her. "I want to be a writer."

"So write."

"How can I if you won't talk with me?"

"I'm talking to you now."

"I could interview you like this, over the phone."

"No, I'd want to see your reaction when I lie to you."

Nick was writing furiously as they talked. For all he knew this was the interview and he intended to make something of it if he had to.

"I'd like to see where you work."

"Look. I'll give you a half hour but it has to be today."

"I'm on my way."

"You better wait until I give you the address."

If he had expected Tara Hall or some other exotic place he would have been disappointed, but he went without prejudice. What difference did it make where a writer lived anyway? Hemingway had settled in different places for shorter or longer times, Fitzgerald had been a rolling stone and so too in a way had Steinbeck. It was the writer who conferred significance on the place, not vice versa. Even so, the old house in an unredeemed part of the city was an unusual place for Rosa Charrin to be working. The frame house needed paint, it had a deserted air about it, and Nick checked the address he had written down before going up and knocking at the door. Knocking. There was no sign of a bell.

When the door opened he was not prepared for her shortness, and her weight. At the library she had seemed mysterious, and striking if not beautiful. But here in a jogging costume and gym shoes that lit up when she walked, short, fat and gimlet-eyed, was Rosa Charrin.

"I'm Nick Byers."

"You were sitting in the back row."

"That's right!"

"With a girl."

"Lucy."

The name gave the little author a start. "Come in, come in."

She took him immediately to her study, and that was more like it. Windowless, some kind of acoustic material on the walls, a trestle table that might have come from Naked Furniture and a massive computer. The screen looked to be 24 inches and the font size of the display was maybe 15. She waved him to a beanbag chair. He plumped down in it and felt at a disadvantage. On the other hand, it was an equalizer. She sat in her swivel chair and brought it around to face him.

"Shoot."

"How long have you been writing?"

He winced as he asked it. For the first ten minutes, all his questions were bad, predictable, and Rosa was getting impatient. Then he decided, the hell with it.

"What would you say if someone called you a hack?"

"What's a hack?"

While he was formulating a definition, she provided one.

"If a hack is someone who writes for money, writes a lot and has a lot of readers, and has them because she has learned her trade and does not repeat herself, I'm a hack."

"Well, given that definition . . ."

"Which fits just about any writer I have any respect for. Ever since writers ran out of royal patrons, they have marketed their own products, well or badly."

"Such as?"

"Dickens, Trollope, Twain, Bierce, the Brontës, Howells . . ."

"Howells?"

"American. William Dean. He's better than he is given credit for."

"I hadn't thought of you as a student of literature."

"I'm not. But I've studied my craft. I write what I write. I am not Edith Wharton or Willa Cather. I am not Joyce Carol Oates. On the other hand, they're not me."

She described the trial and error method by which she had taught herself to write. In half an hour she gave more useful advice to an aspiring writer than Miss McManus could in a year.

"Tell me about Lucy."

Nick shook his head. "Do you know what happened the night we came to hear you?"

"Are you sure you want to tell me?"

"No, this was awful. When she woke up the next morning she found that her grandfather was missing. He has Alzheimer's and apparently wandered away from the house when no one was looking. They're still looking for him."

"I haven't seen anything in the paper."

"That's because no one has found him."

"Lucy could have made an appeal."

"The police advise her to be patient."

"The police?"

"He has been reported as a missing person."

"What did you say his name was?"

"His name is Chester Yates. They all call him Grandpa."

"All?"

"Lucy, her aunt and uncle. Her aunt and uncle live with her. They moved in after Lucy's mother died. It's a long story."

"It sounds like it."

"Funny, her uncle was there for your talk too. He said you once worked at Thompson's."

"Fred Huff?"

"You remember him?"

"He bought a book and I signed it. He reminded me that I had worked at Thompson's."

5

In the middle of a sleepless night Edna stared at the ceiling mottled with lights reflected and refracted from everywhere as if the night meant to squeeze every reflection from the shreds of illumination available. Why hadn't she left well enough alone? What had she expected to gain from leaving Grandpa in the parking lot of the mall in West Toledo? The ceiling was a screen that refused to focus and clarify. Edna had the terrified feeling that she had set in motion something that would bring to an end the comfortable life she and Fred had found here. The worst aspect of her plight was that she did not dare even tell Fred what she had done.

Fred had changed, she wasn't sure how. He was in the house but not of it, holding himself aloof. Of course his work absorbed most of his time and that was good. Finally things seemed to be going well. If they had stayed in Toledo their life would have improved, the apartment had been more than adequate for their needs, no cause to move just because Fred's sales were now more numerous. But then he seemed to work night and day.

Would she have done what she had with Grandpa if Fred had been home that night? Of course she would, what was coming over her? It had always been her lot to be the decisive one, to make a move while others sat on their hands. Edna could not believe that Fred and Lucy did not really think of

Grandpa as she herself did. Let Lucy mope and act as if it was
the end of the world, she was getting a taste of what her life
could be without the albatross of Grandpa around her neck.
And Fred thought what she thought.

Of course it was unnerving not knowing what that crazy
old man had done when she left him there in the parking lot.
No doubt he had wandered off, into the relative wilderness
surrounding the mall. Eventually he would be found, in a
field, in a ditch. She thought these thoughts unflinchingly.
Vivian had died in the hospital, what difference did it make if
Grandpa died in the out-of-doors? Either way, one was dead.
It was silly to think that death was only sad in certain circumstances. But Grandpa's death would not be sad. He would
not be mourned as Vivian was, as a younger person would be.
Funerals of the aged seldom call forth tears. Thus did she rec-
oncile herself to the thought that Grandpa lay already dead in
the vicinity of the mall.

Of course finding him would raise questions she had not
really confronted when she acted. How had the old man
gotten to the mall? If anyone became curious, it would come
out that only Edna had been home with him that night.
Would one of the neighbors claim to have seen her drive away
with Grandpa? Would the car rented in Lucy's name turn attention on her niece or on herself? After all, Lucy had been in
Toledo listening to a lecture. And so apparently had Fred.

"I thought you were working."

"I was lucky to get to the lecture. I told you the woman
used to work at Thompson's, before she got famous."

"Famous!"

"She's come a long way."

"From what?"

"You would have had to know her in those days."

"You never mentioned her before."

"Well, now she's famous."

"Did she remember you?"

"She seemed to."

One thing, if Fred had been home he could have been some help getting her car going after she brought the rental car back to the airport. Her gas tank was bone dry and the airport was all but deserted. She looked toward the exit of the parking lot and the illuminated pay booths. Edna threaded her way among the cars and approached a booth in which an elderly woman was in attendance. Edna approached slowly, in the light, so as not to scare the woman.

"Yes?" She had frightened her after all. What was a woman her age doing sitting in a booth in the middle of the night?

"I'm out of gas."

"Where are you parked?"

"In short term."

"Was there gas in the car when you parked it?"

"Do people steal gas?"

"It has happened."

There was a can of gasoline behind the first booth. Edna had to pay for the gas and put down a deposit on the can. She felt as if she was walking on air as she headed back to her car with the gasoline. The gas splashed into the empty tank. Would a gallon be enough?

Once the gas was in Edna slid behind the wheel and turned the key. There was a grinding sound but the engine did not start. Edna had a very imperfect understanding of the internal combustion engine, but she did understand that the tank was in the rear of the car and the engine in front. Obviously the gas had to make a considerable journey. Angered, Edna opened the door and stepped out, then she stood where a running board would once have been and began to bounce her car up and down. If nothing else, the activity gave her something to do. When she tried again to start the car, it sputtered into life.

At the pay booth, the woman told her she must bring back the gas can full. Edna agreed, but of course she had no intention of running such an errand. She was desperate to get home before Lucy returned, or Fred. But she had waited and waited for someone to come home so she could make the announcement. Grandpa was gone! As it was, the news had to wait until morning.

The odd thing was that Edna had slept like a baby that night.

6

Rosa had learned more from Nick the boy reporter than he had learned from her. The name Lucy could have been a coincidence but from the time he mentioned his girlfriend's name Rosa was sure there was a connection with the old man she had rescued from the parking lot in West Toledo.

Rescued. She liked that. It redeemed so many acts in the past. That night she had been drawn there because of her guilty memories of Julius Sweeney. A little act of expiation that had put her on the scene to witness the abandonment of Grandpa. By Nick's account, Lucy loved the old man and was shattered by his disappearance. It would have been a simple thing to take Grandpa home.

Several things militated against this.

Rosa loved her privacy, and her venture to meet a fraction of her public in the auditorium of the public library in Toledo had satisfied any desire she had for that kind of fame. She would not risk that privacy now, not even for Grandpa.

Perhaps as important as that was the aunt, Edna, who had to be the woman who dropped Grandpa off in the night in a strange place. Rosa made it her mission to make sure that Edna paid for what she had done. Her own deeds seemed by comparison peccadilloes. Well, that was too much, but there was a cruelty about what had been done to Grandpa that Rosa felt was absent from her own acts. True, she had killed several men but even in retrospect that seemed justified. And, after all, she had set Julius free unharmed.

Grandpa was different; he was male but not in a way that mattered anymore. Her rescuing him had been altruistic and keeping him had continued the benevolence. He had been sitting quietly upstairs in her room while she talked with Nick in the study. He would never know that he owed his interview with her to the fact that he had mentioned his girlfriend's name.

It was pleasant to speculate on how she would punish Aunt Edna. She felt she knew the woman all too well. Nick had been eager to pass on to her details of Lucy, her tragedies, her dreadful aunt, her devotion to her grandfather. Through the narrative Edna emerged as the evil presence, the malevolent aunt, the self-righteous Pharisee. The more Rosa reflected on what she had heard of the woman, the more certain she was that Edna had no redeeming features. She was a leech, she was a bully and a nag, she lacked the milk of human kindness. Rosa was sure that Edna had left a trail sufficient to incriminate her. But even if that were true, action on it would take time, if she were accused and indicted, there was the prospect of a trial and the chance that a jury would respond to the disinclination to take care of an elderly relative, particularly one suffering from Alzheimer's. No, justice was both slow and unsure. Rosa resolved to appoint herself judge, jury and executioner.

Meanwhile, she would acquaint herself with the guilty one so that the means chosen would be commensurate with both the crime and the criminal. Step one was talking with Fred Huff.

This proved more difficult than she had supposed. He was never at Thompson's when she called and she declined to have him notified on his beeper that she was trying to reach him.

"I could leave a note."

"No, thank you. I'll call again."

But repeated calls failed to find him in the office. Rosa's memory of Fred Huff was of the slow ball among the salesmen, one who hung on precariously. Her inability to reach him suggested that he had become an ace salesman in the interim. Except that when she studied the literature Thompson's put out, photographs of their sales force as well as houses, the hot shot salesmen were singled out for special attention, and Fred was not among them. Rosa thought of the man who had identified himself when he presented a copy of her book for autographing. She would not have recognized him as the Fred she had known, he had lost his hangdog look, but then he was obviously seeing a similar transformation in her. The runt of the litter had won the blue ribbon.

She took Grandpa with her when she drove over to Toledo to find out what Fred was up to. The expression she remembered from their encounter at her library appearance was knowledgeable and worldly. Fred? And Fred married to the woman Rosa had been learning so much about? Her curiosity was piqued.

She had gleaned from Nick's narrative the time that Fred began his long commute and like the third little pig she started earlier so that she and Grandpa were positioned to watch him when he arrived at the realtor's office. Ten minutes later he left. Rosa followed him to the mall in West Toledo.

She glanced anxiously at Grandpa, but it was silly to think he would remember what had happened to him. Did he even remember Lucy and his life under the tyrannical Edna? Most likely not. Fred parked and sauntered toward one of the entrances, clearly not a man in a hurry.

"Let's go, Grandpa."

No need to persuade him. Rosa wanted to think that there was something more than dumb trust in the way Grandpa responded to her. Maybe he lived in the moment, but she was there in that moment and that was good enough for her.

Fred settled into one of the fast food places, in a booth that had apparently been kept empty for him. He took some things out of his briefcase, for all the world as if this was his office. He was waited on by the manager, who then slid into the bench opposite him and leaned toward him. Fred in a seigniorial gesture touched his fingers to his lips and then brought them to hers. Well.

Fred's obvious ease with the woman, a not too prepossessing female, suggested friendship at least, but the kiss had made it clear that more was going on. Fred's lady friend seemed a first installment on the comeuppance awaiting Edna.

Rosa sat with Grandpa on a bench near the fountain. The constantly flowing water seemed to soothe him. Is that what he might have done if she had not rescued him, in the morning gone inside and sat by the fountain with all the other old people? But they had their minds, if not intact then in reasonably good repair. A few days experience had convinced Rosa that Grandpa was around the bend for good, so far as ever knowing who or where or what he was. From their bench, Rosa could see Fred and the woman manager of the restaurant. They looked to be settled in for hours. Was this how Fred spent his days? Rosa was sure of it. Check into the office, then on to the mall at West Toledo to be greeted by his friend. There was the possibility that he had several such liaisons going in different places, but Rosa doubted it. If Fred had taken the primrose path of dalliance with the woman, it apparently had developed into an almost domestic relationship.

"Like us," she said to Grandpa, digging him in the ribs.

In writing a story, Rosa was in control of the plot, more or less, sometimes things just developed without her being in on it, but for the most part she was in charge. The real events in which she had become involved were another kettle of fish entirely. Those episodes in her past life that she preferred not to dwell upon because they represented her outcast state as a female, had not presented this kind of difficulty, mainly because she was the only one involved who knew what was going to happen. But here there was a relatively large cast of actors:

Grandpa, of course, though you couldn't call him an actor; rather he was the thrown pebble that sent out ever widening circles. He had fallen ill and been lucky to have a daughter-in-law happy to take him into her home. But the daughter-in-law died and that brought in:

Lucy, who had at least as much devotion to Grandpa as her mother had, so things might have gone on unchanged so far as the old man was concerned.

Edna, the aunt, now moves in, along with her seemingly obsequious husband, with designs on the house, perhaps, when Lucy marries and moves out, but of course that would leave Edna and Fred with Grandpa on their hands. No need to wait to solve that little problem. Edna drives Grandpa to West Toledo and dumps him in the parking lot of the mall.

Enter **Rosa** to the rescue. She had swung by the mall on her return to Fort Elbow from her talk at the public library in Toledo, drawn to the mall where she had mercifully released Julius Sweeney after keeping him as an increasingly unwilling guest in her home. Considering the fates earlier male guests had met, Rosa felt understandably magnanimous when she remembered Julius. In any event, there she was, brooding in the mall parking lot, in a position to witness what had happened to Grandpa. At the time she had understood little of what was going on, of course, but she could be forgiven if she felt that someone had delivered Julius back to her. What she got was an elderly man with Alzheimer's, an old man she had grown fond of.

Fred, wife of Edna, had known her in her humiliating days at Thompson's, his excuse for showing up at her talk and having a book signed.

Much of this she had learned when **Nick** interviewed her. Rosa felt sorry for Lucy, worried to death about her Grandpa, and wished she could think of some way to let her know that all was well with the old man. Lucy was computer literate and doubtless had an e-mail address, but a message sent would have a return address so Rosa could not take this means and remain anonymous. A phone call? She did not rule it out.

But Rosa's feelings about Edna trumped any she had about Lucy. The woman had to pay for what she had done. Rosa did not conceal from herself that Edna might thus serve as scapegoat for her own misdeeds, but that did not lessen her resolve to bring the woman to justice, or at least to punish her.

If Edna could be dealt with as she deserved, a bonus for Fred would be a clear path with the woman in West Toledo, if that is what he wanted. He must certainly want freedom from Edna. Let the happy endings proliferate. Nick marries Lucy, Grandpa is restored to his rightful guardian, and Rosa could get the hell back to writing novels.

This plot over which she had little or no control was diverting her from those over which she did.

7

Fred was sure that Edna knew more about the disappearance of Grandpa than she let on. It would have been like her to engineer it and then pretend surprise. After her open annoyance with the old man, expressed when Lucy too could have heard, Edna's current display of broken heartedness was phony as could be. Not that Fred would put the direct question to Edna. He did discuss the disappearance with Hazel but of course he could not mention Edna since the fiction between them was that he had no wife. Even so there was a real if limited satisfaction in discussing the matter with Hazel. It was as if he wanted to get it on the public record that he himself had felt no ill will toward the old man.

"My wife did."

"Your wife?"

"My late wife."

Hazel subsided. Was she getting the spousal urge again? She had assured him she never meant to marry again and that made him feel less exploitative. Did she have any idea how much their afternoons meant to him? He had used Grandpa as his excuse when the suggestion came that he spend the night rather than pop off and go home like a husband. It occurred to him that the disappearance of Grandpa left him vulnerable to Hazel's desire that theirs be more than a day-time thing. How chaste they had become though. Fred had never liked to remember his honeymoon with Edna; it had been his first real experience with her dominating ways. Her reaction to his lovemaking had rendered him all but impotent. But his salad days with Hazel were fresh in his memory, though they inspired an almost disbelief that the two of them had gone at it so hot and heavy. Hazel seemed satisfied that passion had become friendship and their bouts in bed less frequent if no less pleasant.

"The poor old man," Hazel said.

"One good thing is that he won't know what is happening to him."

"How do we know what they know?"

"It is Lucy you should feel sorry for."

"Oh I do, I do. I wish I could meet her."

"Some day. I told you how obsessed with her studies she is."

In the end, he could have derived almost as much consolation talking with a fellow salesman as with Hazel on this matter. In a way, more, because he had to keep what he said to Hazel within the parameters of the description of his life he had given her.

He could talk to Rosa Subiaco, though. Fred had been surprised at the knowledge of human nature she had shown in her talk. The novel he had bought was not his cup of tea, but he gave it to Hazel and she was ecstatic.

"You know her?"

"We worked together years ago."

"Before you were married?"

Fred feigned to think it over. "No, it was afterward." Hazel would have been pardoned if she thought he was lying. Yes, he was sure he could tell Rosa everything, she knew he was married, he could tell her of his suspicions of Edna and it would go no further.

★ ★ ★ ★ ★

"I can't tell you how many people have asked me for that information."

Victor Armitage smiled smugly at Fred who had thought it was an inspiration to seek Rosa's address from the man who had introduced her at the library when he could not get her phone number in any of the usual ways.

"We worked together."

"One woman claimed to be her cousin."

Fred ignored this. "At Thompson's Realty."

"Rosa said she had never heard of her."

"So you do talk with her."

"Of course."

Victor worked until five, after which the library was in the hands of staff. Fred dropped by the library during the dinner hour and took the stairway to the floor where Victor's office was. He was not surprised to find it unlocked. All the offices were darkened now. The Rolodex that had fascinated Fred when he had been condescended to by Victor was still on the desk. He took it to the window where an outside light enabled him to read it. There was no entry under S. Disappointment was bitter, until he tried C. Charrin, Rosa. Fred had half a mind to remove the card and take it with him, but then Victor might put two and two together. He entered the number into his pocket notebook; there was no address.

"Fred?" she asked querulously when he called her the next day.

"Fred Huff. Thompson's. You signed one of your books for me at your talk."

"I remember. How did you get my phone number?"

"It's a secret."

"This is an unlisted number."

"Look, I know all that. This is a big imposition and I realize it. It's just that, listening to you the other night made me sure that you were someone I could talk to about an awful thing that has happened."

"I am not a counselor."

Everything she said was a put-down yet Fred had the odd feeling that he was making progress. After all, she could just hang up if she wanted to.

She said, "It doesn't do my ego any good to be reminded of Thompson's Realty."

That seemed to be the turning point. She asked what the awful thing was and answered with a question, "Have you ever lost anyone?"

It came down to where they could talk. He was startled when she proposed the mall in West Toledo.

"Why there?"

"It's closer than Toledo."

"Oh, I'm not suggesting that you drive all the way over here. I can meet you in Fort Elbow."

"I don't mind driving to West Toledo."

"I wouldn't hear of it."

For some damned reason she insisted, and when he agreed he told himself they could keep away from Hazel. Only Hazel could be jealous of someone like Rosa. He would pass Rosa off as a client in search of a house.

8

It was a woman's voice and she took so long before saying anything, just breathing audibly, that Edna thought it might be an obscene phone call but she kept it to her ear out of curiosity.

"I know what you did."

"Who is this?"

"Grandpa is safe."

"Grandpa!"

"And you are going to pay."

The connection was broken. Edna could not put down the phone for minutes, half expecting that more terrifying words would emerge from it. My God! This was worse than her worst fears. And she had called him Grandpa. How could she know that was what they called him?

Finally she got rid of the phone but she sat staring sightlessly ahead. The call made no sense. No one could know what she had done. But no sooner did she tell herself that than she thought of all those who might have told the police things—the girl at the rental car counter, the woman in the pay booth at the airport. She might resent not getting her gas can back. Edna had stowed it in the garage, since it filled her trunk with the stench of gas. But it was not the police who called.

Edna told herself it was a trick that Lucy was playing on her. That had to be it. Edna smiled cruelly. Her mistake had been in calling him Grandpa. Only someone who lived in this house would call him that. Edna nodded, her lips now forming a thin line of resolution. She would not mention the call. Whatever satisfaction Lucy had sought to derive from pulling such a trick would not be forthcoming. She could wait until doomsday before she learned from Edna of the call.

She kept a close eye on her niece after the call, looking for any sign that she was responsible, but there was none. Edna began to regard her suspicions as ridiculous. Lucy was really broken up over Grandpa's disappearance and would have been incapable of playing such games about it. Who then? How she wished she had demanded to know what the caller wanted. If it was someone who thought they could blackmail her about it, well, Edna would inform the police. Perhaps she should tell them of this call.

She jumped to her feet. Yes, that was the ticket. The police would know what to do. But the police meant Lieutenant Noonan. Lucy had talked with a woman officer named Kuss, but when Edna herself went to Missing Persons, to reinforce the urgency of getting the old man back, Lieutenant Noonan had been on duty.

"Is he on medication?"

"There is no medication for Alzheimer's."

"Any other medication. I mean. Is he in danger?"

"And what if he was?"

"How do you mean?"

"Could you get his medication to him?"

Noonan got the message. She thought he was stupid. She would have to hope someone else would be on duty.

But it was Noonan who looked up when she entered Missing Persons. It astounded Edna that so many persons were lost that it required a special division.

"Oh, not many are really lost," Noonan said, glancing at

the half-done crossword on his desk. "Most just took a powder, divorced husbands, boyfriends, children."

He acted as if half the world was hiding from the other half. On this second visit, she went straight to the point.

"I got a strange phone call."

He just sat there, staring at her stupidly. How she would have liked to ask to speak to his superior.

"A woman's voice telling me that Grandpa was all right."

"What do they want?"

"That was all. She hung up after saying that."

"That Grandpa was all right?"

"Yes."

"She called him Grandpa?"

Edna had thought of this on the way downtown. How could she know we called him that?

"Of course she didn't call him Grandpa."

"What did she call him?"

"He? Maybe she said the old man."

"You don't remember."

"I am telling you what I remember." Edna remained calm. Why did she think that this ass was trying to provoke her?

"Do you remember the time of the call?"

"I came here immediately. It was within the hour."

Noonan nodded, and first brought his hands together and then lifted his fingertips to his chin. "Very interesting. It sounds like a kidnapping whether or not they've asked for anything yet. Of course they'll know you came here."

"How?"

He shrugged. "We have to assume they do."

He was telling her she had done something stupid. She couldn't agree more. This was a huge mistake. If she had left well enough alone, Grandpa's disappearance would have gotten lost among all the other lost persons.

"Of course they might have known if you only called here."

"I did."

"But then they know you reported him missing. Or your niece did."

Everything he said had an edge to it, yet he was the most expressionless person she had ever met. She did not like the thought of such a person seriously investigating Grandpa's disappearance. He seemed a slothful toad, but she had the impression he could be unrelenting if he had a lead to follow.

"It probably won't do any good but we can put a tap on your phone," Noonan said.

How could she object?

"What does your niece make of this?"

Edna said, "I wanted to ask you if I should tell her."

"Why wouldn't you?"

"It will raise her hopes."

"It can't do any harm to tell her that he is all right."

"Can we believe her? I mean the caller."

"We'll see."

Lucy was elated when told the news, asking for the message to be repeated over and over, and when Edna rephrased it she demanded to know what it was exactly, so Edna stayed with what she had told Noonan. The old man is all right, don't worry.

"Oh, thank God, thank God. How did they know who to call?"

"That is what Lieutenant Noonan wonders."

"You were right to tell him right away." And Lucy embraced her, pressing her lips to Edna's sprayed hair. Then she stepped back. "They must have found one of the labels in his clothes."

"Of course!" But Edna knew that all the tags had been removed. She had done that herself. Still, it provided an explanation of the call.

"And there is the lottery ticket, but that would have been no help."

"Lottery ticket!"

Lucy looked embarrassed. "I told him it was ours, his and mine, we would split the fortune. It's for the Power Ball on Saturday night. Whenever it goes above fifty million, I buy a ticket."

"He didn't have it with him."

"Oh yes. It is in the handkerchief pocket of his corduroy jacket. He must have been wearing it, it's not in his closet."

Edna had not checked that pocket, why would she? In any case, as Lucy said, it was absurd to think that a lottery ticket was an identification card.

9

Nick showed Lucy a draft of the piece on Rosa Charrin and she read it with great attention. As she did, Nick tried to distract himself. He wandered down the hall and looked into the room Lucy's grandfather had occupied. This was the room Edna had found empty that morning and flew to wake Lucy with the dreadful news. Nick stepped into the room and stood there. Seized with a momentary superstition, he closed his eyes and invited the room to tell him what had happened to Grandpa. "Tell me where he is now," he murmured. "For Lucy's sake."

The telephone call had given Lucy an inflated hope that rapidly deflated when she had heard of Lieutenant Noonan's reaction. But at least they knew that the old man was still alive, if the caller had been telling the truth. But of course they didn't know that. Maybe nametags had provided a basis for the calls, but that only meant that someone had found Grandpa's clothes. Why hadn't they asked for something?

"What are you doing?"

Nick wheeled to face Edna, who stood in the doorway of the bedroom as if prepared to block his escape.

"Nothing."

"That will not do. What are you doing here in Grandpa's room?"

Lucy, drawn by the fuss, came to his rescue. "He is waiting for me to finish reading this." She shook the pages at her aunt then turned to Nick with a quite different expression. "Nick, this is good!"

"What is it?" Edna demanded.

"Nick's feature story on Rosa Charrin."

"Oh brother, Rosa Charrin," Edna said, and left them alone.

"We are all so keyed up, Nick. She didn't mean anything."

That was like Lucy, giving others the benefit of the doubt, but Nick had felt a hatred emanating from Edna as she stood in the doorway.

They went off to have a few beers and talk about what he had written. Lucy's reaction had only confirmed Nick's certainty that he had put together a fully professional piece. Ahead lay the great adventure of submitting it to a newspaper.

"Why shouldn't I try to sell it in Fort Elbow?"

"That's a great idea."

"If they don't want it, I can then go to Toledo with it."

"The *Fort Elbow Tribune* will want it."

"Do you want to be my agent?"

But their thoughts soon returned to Grandpa, dragged back by the memory of Edna's angry outburst at the house.

"What bothers me the most is the way the police are handling it. Or not handling it. For them, missing persons are a daily event, there is a new bunch of reports every morning. They have a routine, one that almost never finds the missing person."

"We have to hope there will be another call."

"I almost think Edna dreamed that call. I could dream it."

"Take comfort in the fact that he is all right."

She nodded, and looked at him sheepishly. "It is so hard to keep my mind on anything else. I told Edna about the lottery ticket and I know she thought I had lost my mind."

"She is on edge."

"I wonder if I should hire someone to look for him."

"A private detective?"

"There are scads of them listed in the Yellow Pages."

Nick let her talk about the possibility, feeling that he was humoring her. It seemed a sign of the desperation to which she had come. On balance, the phone call only made it worse. As soon as you thought of the possibility that it was some kind of cruel hoax, the harder it was to dismiss it.

"I mentioned it to Rosa. Because she knows Fred."

"Fred," Lucy said, and her tone said volumes of what she thought of her henpecked uncle.

"Rosa signed a book for him."

"He never mentioned it."

"Maybe he'll give it to you."

"I'll ask."

He did not tell Lucy that knowing where Rosa lived had prompted him to drive over there and park, looking at the house, absorbing its atmosphere as he had tried to absorb that of Grandpa's room. He parked up the street from her house for several hours, until people began to walk by slowly and look in at him, wondering what he was up to. In that neighborhood, a stranger in a parked car could spell menace. Nick had driven slowly away. But he had put into his story a reason why Rosa was so jealous of her privacy. Fans would converge on the house and make it impossible for her to write.

10

Lucy had mentioned the lottery ticket to Edna but had not really thought about it since. On Sunday morning, Edna said, "Well, there are the winning numbers. I wonder if Grandpa won."

Lucy took cognizance of her aunt's sardonic remark, but did not ask to see the section of the Sunday paper in which the winning numbers were printed. It was an hour later that, sitting in her own room, she opened to the page with the lottery results. She had written the numbers of the ticket in the little notebook in which she jotted down things going on at the university. She lay the little book open on her pillow and then looked down at the row of numbers, beginning at the end. The Power Ball number. 6. She glanced at her notebook. 6! Her breath caught, that meant the ticket was worth at least something. But then she traced backward through the numbers, slowly, then more slowly, no longer breathing. The numbers continued to match! They all matched. My God, she and Grandpa had won the Power Ball. The amount listed brought her slowly to her feet. Fifty-six million dollars.

She was about to run into the kitchen and tell her aunt, but stopped before she got to the door. What good were the numbers if the ticket was lost? The ticket was wherever Grandpa was. Knowing that there had been a lottery ticket worth such a king's ransom would only make things worse.

A king's ransom.

Lucy got out the telephone directory and opened the Yellow Pages to the listing of private detectives. How could one make a rational choice of such unknowns? She should consult Alex. But she could predict his reaction. Leave it to the police, they are doing everything that can be done. And they would resent it if they knew she had hired a detective. Their reaction could well be, okay, let the private detective find the old man. It would be a vote of no confidence in the police, that is how they would see it.

But Lucy had no confidence in them. She could approach a detective and, depending on whether she had confidence in him, let him know about the lottery. The prospect of that kind of money would be incentive enough and she need not depend on Alex for the money to hire him.

Him? There were women private detectives, as she had noticed to her astonishment. No, she wanted a man. Images of Humphrey Bogart came and went, the black and white films she and Nick had laughed over in the student union.

She closed her eyes and her lips moved as if in prayer. Then she pointed at the page. She opened her eyes. Her index finger was square in the middle of a boxed ad. Norman Earwick. Investigations.

Part Three

SCRATCH

1

In what billed itself as a satellite of the mall on whose outskirts it parasitically stood was a building called the Phoenix in which the offices of Norman Earwick were located. The Phoenix arose as if from the ashes of its developers hopes and seemed shouldered aside by a low flat complex featuring the China Express whose all-you-can-eat buffet had added more to the avoirdupois of Earwick than he had added to the coffers of John Wu the proprietor. There was also a drop-off store of Zither's Dry Cleaning, a computer store, and an ill-lit place whose flashing lights and odd noises sufficed to identify it as devoted to Games, and Venter's, one of a local chain of 24-hour supermarkets. To park in the lot devoted to these enterprises was to risk the temporary loss of one's vehicle but there was, behind the Phoenix, a thinly surfaced irregularly shaped lot, two designated locations of which were cryptically identified as Earwick Investigations.

The eponymous Earwick occupied a suite on the second and top floor of the Phoenix reached by elevator, inside stairway and, suggestively, an outside stairway that rose from the parking lot. Etymologically, suite signifies sequence, that which follows, the linear arrangement of whatever. In the case in question it designated two moderately sized rooms, in the first of which was ensconced Mrs. Barnacle, the latest optimist to cast her lot with Earwick. The second room was the office of Norman Earwick. There was—oh, luxury—a wash-room as well, access to which was contested by employer and employee.

"Miss Lucy Yates," Mrs. Barnacle announced, when she had buzzed her investigative employer after answering the phone.

"What about her?"

"She wants to speak with you."

"What about?"

Into this supposedly confidential exchange, a third voice intervened. "I want to hire you."

"Who's that?" Earwick demanded.

"Damn," cried Mrs. Barnacle. "I can't get the hang of this phone. You are on with Mr. Barnacle, Miss."

In this inauspicious way was Earwick first put into contact with Lucy Yates. She was loath to divulge on the phone the nature of her interest in his services and wanted very much to see him as soon as possible. Such eagerness was a novelty in the Earwick suite and he became wary.

"Who recommended me?"

"I saw your ad in the phone book."

"There are many ads in the phone book."

"Would you like me to try someone else?"

"Not at all. Are you free this morning?"

"I am."

"Having seen my ad, you know the location of my offices."

"I could come now."

"Are you still on the line, Mrs. Barnacle?" She wasn't. "Very well. Come along and I will fit you in."

Having hung up, he debated the wisdom of chiding Mrs. Barnacle about her ineptitude. Arguing against that was the fact that she made very good coffee. On the other hand, she did not take dictation. But, for that matter, he had not had anything to dictate to her since she had come aboard. He had told her to put order into the files, a pointless task that would keep her occupied until something turned up. Was that something Miss Lucy Yates?

Norman Earwick had not lived into his fifty-seventh year without becoming acquainted with the rise and fall of fortune. Many considered such fluctuations unpredictable. Sadly, Norman was all too capable of predicting them. But dark days had not dashed his congenital optimism. A stint in the military police during the two years he referred to somewhat solemnly as his war experience had given him a taste for law enforcement. On returning to civilian life, he had taken the exam and been admitted to the police academy and was eventually graduated and taken onto the force. In those days, it was rare for a candidate to be rejected, jobs elsewhere being plentiful.

Norman had loved police work. His nickname, Norm, seemed to make him a custodian of the law, the rule of conduct, the normal. He had held his head high, not merely to erase the incipient double chin, but in genuine pride that he stood on the side of law and order and justice. In the Army, the foe had been a declared enemy, by definition bent on destroying the foundations of civilized society. For the police, there were battles but no war, and it was an endless struggle, new recruits on both sides entering the fray, replacing their retired or imprisoned predecessors. Norm had left the army feeling the same patriotism and devotion with which he had entered. His love affair with law and order had a different upshot.

It was Norm's fate to be appointed to the internal investigation division right out of the academy. He felt disappointment that he would not be seen on the streets of the city wearing his uniform; as it turned out he was never to wear a uniform on duty. The task of IID was to ferret out those members of the force who were on the take, who used the uniform as the best disguise for covert criminal activity. Norm would have supposed that such bad apples were rare in the barrel and he was shocked by the number of cases that came before them. There were accusations, there were hearings, reprimands were issued.

"Why don't we throw the book at them?" Norm demanded. "They are traitors. Judases."

His neophyte zeal was tolerantly indulged. Gradually it became clear to Norm that IID was not the enemy of the bad cop, but his advocate, the aim was to clear the officer. Nor was this merely an expression of esprit de corps, the spirit of forgiveness or mercy. Those who did go down were those too stupid or stubborn to interpret the hints given them. The conduct that had brought the officer before the board might continue on another basis, if the miscreant shared the wealth.

Norm's disillusionment was total. He felt betrayed. To his newly baleful eye the courts seemed as corrupt as the police. What he had regarded as the eternal struggle between good and evil was just a game and people played on whichever team stood the best change of winning. Cops, lawyers, judges, all of them. Where was rectitude to be found? He might have gotten religion but for the clerics who turned up in raids on unsavory places. At the age of thirty, the scales had fallen from his eyes. He was ready for the real world.

He resigned from the force and got a private investigator's license. He preferred being a freelancer than one more gun in the equivocal forces of justice. Low as his hopes had been when he set up shop, disillusionment of another sort came in his new career as well. His clientele were by definition those with a grievance, sometimes genuine. Broken homes, beaten wives, rotten kids, drugs, booze, money—Norm's sense of universal depravity rivaled John Calvin's. But it was in this fallen world that he must make his living, and he had. His youthful idealism had eroded until there was nothing less but cynicism. For a PI, this was like passing the bar exams.

"I want to hire you to find a missing person," Lucy Yates said, when Mrs. Barnacle had ushered her into the office. On her way out, Mrs. Barnacle pointedly opened a window to let out the stale cigar smoke. Lucy was younger than he would have expected.

"I thought so."

"You thought so!"

"You're too young to have a runaway child, in fact you're not even married, unless your rings are in your purse. It can't be divorce. Who's missing?"

"My grandfather."

"Ah."

"He has Alzheimer's. He lives with me. Five days ago he just disappeared."

Norman shook his head. "People don't disappear. It's physically impossible."

"He's gone then and I am worried sick . . ." Her voice trembled and Norman waited to see if she would cry. Clients usually cried, or raged with anger: the tears and rage of those who had been done to before they could do to. But she did not lose control.

"Tell me all about it."

It could become a new genre of client, these cases were becoming frequent enough. Where had Alzheimer's come from anyway? Norm had never heard of it when he was young. People now lived long enough to go gaga, that was one explanation, then again it might be something toxic we had put into circulation, like tobacco and booze. The unreported cases of missing seniors whose sense of reality had gone were the ones in which a relative had tried to lose the burdensome person. Norm had a folder somewhere in his file cabinets, clippings of abandoned elders who didn't know who or where they were.

"I haven't read about it."

"It hasn't been in the papers."

"Why not?"

"The police advised against it."

"Missing Persons?"

"Lieutenant Noonan."

Involuntarily, Norman made a sound of disgust.

"Do you know him?"

"Let's just say I am glad you came to me. Noonan couldn't find his rear end with both hands." He was startled by her laughter. "No need to seek the missing link, it's Noonan."

It was rare for a client to be amused by what he said, and Norman wasn't sure he liked it. Laughter at his words could too easily be directed at the speaker.

"You realize that, unlike the police, I am not paid by your taxes."

"There is something else I should tell you."

"Yes."

"Grandpa has last week's winning Power Ball ticket."

"Last week's!"

"Yes."

"But that was worth . . ."

"Fifty-six million dollars."

Of course Norm did not believe the girl, however much she apparently believed herself. Still, it was an interesting way to try to hire someone.

"And you're offering to share it with me if we find Grandpa."

"Oh no. I will pay your usual fee. And a bonus, I suppose, given all that money."

"If he has the ticket how do you know it's the winning ticket?"

"I wrote down the numbers when I bought it for him. For us. I told him we would go halfsies."

"You told him. He understood you?"

"In his way. Here." She pushed an open notebook across the desk to him, pointing to the row of numbers written there. Of course anyone could know those numbers now. Norman wrote them down anyway. This was becoming mildly interesting.

"The aunt and uncle you mentioned, do they know you have come here?"

"Oh no. Edna wouldn't like it. Fred might. But it has to be a secret."

She would have thought the same thing that occurred to Norman, the aunt and uncle were responsible. Perhaps Miss Lucy Yates wanted to win the daily double: get Grandpa back and get rid of aunt and uncle. He told her he would accept her as a client.

"Fill out a form with Mrs. Barnacle."

"Did you know James Joyce's wife was Nora Barnacle?"

"Who's he?"

"An Irishman."

"Mrs. Barnacle is Jewish. Her maiden name was Schwartz."

A harmless lie. Who the hell was James Joyce?

2

Had she done the wrong thing? Norman Earwick was not what Mrs. McManus would call prepossessing. Of course it didn't matter that he didn't know who James Joyce was. Edna and Fred probably didn't know either. It was a burden to give all the details of Grandpa's disappearance to someone other than Lieutenant Noonan and she was sick and tired of going over and over it with Aunt Edna. Edna was like a melting iceberg, having drifted from the cold climes in which she had lived her life into these warmer waters of loss and helplessness. Lucy scolded herself for ever having doubted Aunt Edna's affection for Grandpa. Would she have moved into the house if she didn't love him? Edna just disguised her emotions behind an icy disapproving veneer. But the veneer had melted and she looked haggard and haunted.

"Don't blame yourself, Aunt Edna."

"What are you talking about!" Edna looked wildly at Lucy.

"We mustn't feel guilty about this, it's not our fault."

"Of course it's not our fault."

She had hoped to soothe her aunt, to embrace her and give her a reassurance she no longer had that the police would find Grandpa. But the days passed and hope was ever more difficult. She was sorely tempted to tell her aunt that now they had the help of their own special investigator to look into the matter.

"You're saying he just walked away one night," Earwick repeated. "Had he done that before?"

"Never. Day or night, he stayed as close as possible to what was familiar to him."

"Your aunt was home alone with him?"

"Yes."

"Had anything special happened that day? Anything out of the ordinary that might have annoyed your aunt?"

"Annoyed my aunt! What's that got to do with it?"

He merely shrugged, but she saw the direction his mind was headed. It was discouraging to think that he would pursue the wrong hunch and waste a lot of time pursuing it. But she had to trust him. She herself had tried to track down Grandpa and that was when the trail was hot. No neighbors had reported seeing him. Obviously he couldn't be in the neighborhood and not be noticed. On the wild hope that he might reappear as mysteriously as he had disappeared, she regularly went through the house from top to bottom. She checked the garage. That was when she noticed the large red gas can.

"How could that have got there?" she asked Edna. The gas for the mower and snow blower was locked in a shed when kept at all. Lucy's mother had been made ill by the smell of gas and was certain they would have a fire with a can of it sitting about.

"Hasn't it always been there?"

"No."

"Well, it has been for some time."

The following day, when Fred brought her home from class, Lucy's eye was caught by the sight of the red gas can set out on the curb with the garbage. She took it out of the plastic bag and brought it back to the garage. Edna should know that such objects had to go out with trash on Tuesday. The re-

111

appearance of the can upset Edna further.

"I put that in the trash and it's back!"

"I brought it back."

"I thought it bothered you, that you thought it a danger."

"It can go out on Tuesday, Aunt Edna. With the trash. You can't put a can like that in the garbage."

"All this fuss about a gas can."

"I wish I knew where it came from."

Edna made an impatient noise and stomped away. Later, when Fred had left, the can was again gone from the garage. Edna said she had taken it to a mall and tossed it into one of the huge trash receptacles there.

"It bothered you. It came to bother me. So I got rid of it."

"I hope it had nothing to do with Grandpa's disappearance."

"What do you mean?"

"I don't know. It wasn't there and then it's there and he's gone." Lucy waved her hand to dismiss these thoughts. "I don't know what to think of anything anymore."

"You're over wrought," Edna said, after a very long time just looking at Lucy. And then she took her awkwardly in her arms, showing an affection Lucy realized she had longed for. "Lie down, dear, take a nap. None of us is getting nearly enough sleep."

The police had seemed lackadaisical when they examined the house and neighborhood, as if they didn't really expect to find anything useful. She had discouraged Norman Earwick from coming to the house, unless she arranged the time. It would have to be when Edna was away.

"The scene is thoroughly contaminated now anyway."

"Contaminated."

"Usually you tape off the scene of such an event, to make

sure that people don't inadvertently—or advertently—destroy evidence or clues as to what might have happened."

"I would be the chief contaminator then. I looked everywhere for some indication of where he had gone."

"When you thought about it, where did you imagine he had gone?"

"That is the strange thing about Alzheimer's. He could feel equally at home or lost anywhere. Only the most immediate environment seems to matter, a sort of bubble in which he lives, cut off from the world."

He did ask for detailed descriptions of what Grandpa was wearing. He asked her to bring him a pair of shoes and trousers. Lucy felt she was dealing with a sorcerer who hoped to conjure up Grandpa by chanting over his clothes. Oh, that wasn't fair. But her second visit to Earwick's office did not inspire total confidence. Mrs. Barnacle seemed to sense Lucy's doubts.

"Don't worry, he always gets his man, or woman. Just when you think it's all over, bingo, he has them."

That was a great relief, until Lucy remembered that Mrs. Barnacle was new at her job.

It was then that a great fantasy began to form in her mind. She had learned too much about how difficult it could be to locate a person who was missing. On the face of it, it seemed impossible for a person simply to disappear. Yet, according to Earwick, people did it all the time. How did they go about it? What if she herself were now to disappear? This would create a stir, put new energy into everyone, police, Earwick, the newspapers. What was most frustrating was the fact that Grandpa's disappearance was like a family secret. Only a few people knew of it, the police had discouraged her from publicizing it. It was as if it had never happened, and time was passing, time when poor Grandpa was very likely in the custody of the woman who had called Edna. The phone was never left unattended. But no further calls came. If Lucy disappeared . . .

Even to think of it was to face huge obstacles. If she took her car, that could be traced. If she abandoned it somewhere, ditto. Where would she stay? A hotel or motel would require her to register. She would have to eat. She realized how many witnesses there were to each of her daily deeds, so that if she did disappear there would be dozens of people who could provide information. That was the great difference with Grandpa, given the solitary life he lived. He had fallen out of touch with the world and vice versa.

"It's back!"

Edna stood before her, hands on her hips, head lowered, an angry expression on her narrow face.

"What's back?"

"You know very well what I'm talking about. You went and fetched it and put it in the garage. I want to know why."

"Edna, I haven't the faintest idea what you are talking about."

"That damned gas can. Why did you go get it?"

"Go get it? I don't know what you did with it."

"I told you. I told you I had put it in a trash receptacle at the mall."

Lucy just looked at her. "And you think that would be enough for me to go get it? Edna, why would I go get that gas can?"

"That is what I want to know."

"But I didn't get it." Lucy stood. "Show me where it is."

In the garage, Edna pulled open the back door of her car and pointed. The gas can was there, lying on its side. "There," Edna said triumphantly. And, when Lucy made a move to take it out, "Leave it alone. I intend to throw it away for good and I will not tolerate your playing games like this."

Whereupon, Edna went around to the driver's door and got behind the wheel. She backed out of the garage much too fast and in the street, turned into traffic to a great complaint of horns. Gears shifted and then she shot away up the street. Lucy realized that her mouth was hanging open. Of all the crazy things.

She and Edna observed an uneasy silence when her aunt returned, and things weren't helped much when Fred came home from Toledo.

The following day the gas can was back in the garage and Edna became hysterical.

3

Fred had never known Edna to act so strangely and he felt he had an odd advantage over her, a very unaccustomed feeling and not one he wholly welcomed. The double life he had been leading since they had moved in with Lucy and he had become friends with Hazel was exciting in large part because of Edna's certain reaction if she ever found out. Her contempt for him was palpable but Fred sensed that this was all the more reason why she could never bear the thought that he had gotten out of her clutches. A scornful woman scorned would be a terrible thing indeed. Now she seemed to have flipped out over a gas can.

He returned to a hushed house and Lucy drew him into the back hallway to tell him what had happened. It was difficult to take seriously. The disappearing and reappearing gas can seemed a sick symbol of Grandpa's disappearance. Fred found that he truly missed the old man. Perhaps he had thought of the two of them as forming a brotherhood, the designated victims of Edna. But he had the great advantage of being able to get out of the way of her petty tyranny, whereas poor Grandpa was utterly helpless. No wonder his first reaction to the news that Grandpa was gone was elation that the old fellow had finally had too much. Lucy seemed to take the gas can as seriously as Edna.

"Where is she?"

"In her room."

Her room. Did Lucy never wonder about this strange marriage?

"I'll go talk to her."

The room was darkened but the figure of his wife upon her solitary bed was visible in the light from the hall. Fred let his eyes become accustomed to the want of light and then pulled the door shut and moved slowly toward the bed. He had miscalculated the distance and bumped against the bed.

Edna rose with a shriek and began to flail about, thrashing the air with her arms, her voice rising into the higher hysterical registers. Fred tried to get hold of her, to calm her, but she swung out wildly and hit him several times before he could grab her arms and hold them.

"God damn it, Edna. Take it easy."

She seemed to collapse at the sound of his voice and her scream became a moaning. Fred let go of her hand and groped for the lamp beside the bed, tipping it over in the process. Edna stiffened but he righted the lamp and turned it on. The ribbed shade was set at a saucy angle but he left it as it was. She was on her knees on the bed, blinking against the light, and then she moved toward him like a penitent at a shrine, her arms reaching for him. She embraced him frantically and began to sob against his shoulder.

"I think I am losing my mind."

His face was aflame where she had struck him and he accepted the embrace as a mode of defense against any renewal of attack. What a contrast between this bedroom and Hazel's scented boudoir where the pleasures of the flesh were ever in the offing. Being actually desired by a woman was such a novel experience that it marked a dramatic contrast with his alleged marriage. Now, for the first time feeling in control of things, Fred wondered why he had not left Edna long ago.

"Tell me about it."

She gave him a disjointed version of what Lucy had told him and he rocked her in his arms.

"Edna, Edna. It's only a gas can."

She struggled free of him and retreated across the bed.

"Is it you? Have you been doing this?"

She was a haggard, terrified woman, Lady MacBeth. Rosa's talk had stirred long dormant interests in Fred, and he had been reading Shakespeare to Hazel.

"My wife was like that," he ventured to say.

"No."

The comparison did not seem fanciful now. It occurred to him that Edna's reaction to the gas can was like Lady Macbeth's to the vision of the dagger.

"No, of course not," he said in response to Edna's accusation. It was an old trick of hers, turning her own misdeed into cause for blaming him. He was suddenly certain that Edna knew what had happened to Grandpa and the conviction bestowed an unusual power on him. But not enough power that he dared express his suspicion of her. Her guilt was producing hallucinations. First, there had been the phone call, a call only Edna had knowledge of. The gas can, on the other hand, Lucy knew of as well. Fred felt a need to sort out his thoughts.

"You have to get some sleep."

"Will you get rid of that can?"

"Yes, yes, of course. Where are your pills?"

"What pills?"

"Your sleeping pills." Were there other pills? It was a bizarre thought that despite their sexless marriage Edna had gone on taking the daily pill that guaranteed her barrenness.

"In the drawer."

He found the bottle and put it on the table. "I'll get some water."

"First get rid of that can."

"Edna, I promise you I will take care of it. But first I want to see you calmed down."

He brought a glass of water, conscious of Lucy darting out of sight when he emerged from the bedroom. Edna still knelt on her bed. Fred handed her the bottle but she had trouble with the cap, one meant to keep its contents safe from children. He pressed down and twisted it open and handed it to her, but she shook her head and held out her hand. As he tipped the opened bottle over her cupped hands, half a dozen pills fell out.

"How many do you take?"

In answer, she brought her hand to her mouth and took them all. When he handed her the water, Fred felt like an accomplice. How many pills spelled danger? They might have been conducting an experiment to find out. She drank the water as if she were dying of thirst and then fell forward onto her pillow. The moaning began again. He sat on the side of the bed, and stroked her shoulders. He ran a hand through her damp grizzled hair. She was not aging gracefully. Five minutes later she was completely relaxed. Fred took away his hand and a moment later got quietly to his feet. He straightened the shade but left the light burning. He shut the door when he left the room.

"How is she?" Lucy asked in a whisper.

"Sleeping. I promised her I would get rid of that can."

"Fred, what difference does it make?"

"To Edna? Obviously a lot."

"But why? I mean, it's strange but she reacted to it the first time the same way. It's coming and going only intensified that. I wish I had told you then."

He could tell that her failure to do so indicated how much help she thought he would be. Again she went through the se-

119

quence of events. Edna had mistakenly put the can out with the garbage and when Lucy retrieved it was furious. She drove off with it and said she threw it in a dumpster at the mall.

"The mall."

"I think she meant the shopping area over on Bryant."

"Lucy, you didn't . . ."

"No."

"But it showed up here again?"

"And she accused me of bringing it back, to annoy her."

Obviously the gas can meant something to Edna and its mysterious comings and goings had, in Lucy's account, intensified her wild reaction to it. In some way that can was connected with Grandpa's disappearance.

"It began with the phone call, Fred."

"If there was a phone call."

A silence fell and the icemaker in the refrigerator was audible. Lucy looked away, as if she did not want to confront the significance of what he had said. Then she turned to him and put her hand on his.

"Fred, there is something else I should have told you."

Fred listened to her account of hiring a private detective to find Grandpa and bring him home. How on earth was she going to pay for such an investigation?

"There is more. I bought a lottery ticket, for me and Grandpa. Fred, it was the winning ticket. It is worth fifty-six millions dollars."

He fell back in his chair and stared at her. One had gotten used to hearing of the enormous sums won in the lottery, but it had never seemed real. Hazel bought twenty dollars worth of lottery tickets every week and she had never won but a few dollars.

"Where is the ticket?"

"Grandpa has it."

"Grandpa!"

His avarice gland had begun to secrete when she first mentioned the amount of money but now Fred felt that impossible riches had just been snatched from him. It went without saying that they would all share in such a bonanza.

"I put it into the top pocket of his corduroy jacket that he was wearing when he disappeared."

"How do you know that?"

"It's not in his closet."

Fred rose and went to Grandpa's room, turned on the light and opened the closet door. He felt around, he peered at the garments, finally he brought them all out and threw them on the bed. Lucy looked on in amazement as he began to search them all.

"He might have transferred it."

Lucy joined in the search, saying she had never thought of that. But there was no trace of the ticket. They hung up Grandpa's clothes, Lucy arranging them neatly and then impulsively burying her face in one of his shirts.

In the kitchen, she showed him the row of numbers in her notebook as well as the notice torn from the paper. It never occurred to Fred to doubt the truth of what she was saying. But that meant a ticket worth all those millions had disappeared with Grandpa. He realized that he was moaning as Edna had.

"Does Edna know of this?"

"I told her of the lottery ticket, but not that it won."

"Maybe you should have."

But he did not want to discuss with Lucy what such information might have precipitated. If Edna knew anything of what had happened to Grandpa, the prospect of all that money would have brought it out.

"Did you tell the detective?"

Lucy nodded and Fred managed not to groan.

"What is his name?"

"Norman Earwick."

4

"What should I do with these clothes?" Mrs. Barnacle asked, indicating the shirt and trousers Lucy had brought.

"The closet."

"Why do you want them?"

"No particular reason. It is important to convey to the client that you are systematically at work."

"What have you found out?"

"All in good time," Norman said slyly. "All in good time."

He closed the door of his office and opened a diet cola and took a deep drink. From a lower drawer, he got out a bottle of bourbon and laced the soda. Then, tipping back in his chair, he sipped meditatively and acknowledged that he had no more idea what had happened to Lucy's grandfather than she did.

It had been more than a week since the old man's disappearance. Norman had made inquiries at the morgue, and there had been one possible, but when he had gone down and looked at the body, fish-belly white with lots of belly, a huge guy and not nearly old enough, he repeated the description to Dewey. Dewey's expression was that of a man who thought that when you have seen one dead body you have seen them all, and Norman had the fleeting thought of passing off a corpse as Grandpa. Bah. That would have been difficult to do in the Middle Ages, but nowadays a person could be identified accurately with a spot of blood, a bit of flesh, let alone dental records and fingerprints. Lawyers might argue about DNA in courts of law, but before you got there it was considered decisive.

The old man hadn't turned up dead so that meant he was still alive. He was incapable of going anywhere on his own, so that meant someone had him in their custody. Someone had allegedly called Edna and assured her that the old man was okay. It was weird and Norman, who dealt in the weird, was baffled. His thoughts turned, as they had before, to the possibility that it was an inside job, when Mrs. Barnacle announced a visitor.

"Mr. Fred Huff," she said, leaning into his just opened door and whispering.

"I don't know him."

"Lucy's uncle."

Norman got into a business like posture, decided against hiding the can of soda, took several sips, and said, "Send him in."

His visitor spoke before getting settled in the chair to which Mrs. Barnacle brought him. "My niece tells me that she has hired you to find her grandfather."

"That's right."

"And she told you about the lottery ticket."

Norman smiled indulgently. "She seemed to think that would motivate me to take the case."

"Did it?"

"What do you know of this lottery ticket?"

"Only what Lucy told me. She had the winning numbers written down."

"But the question arises, when did she write them down, before or after the announcement?"

Fred sat in silence. "Of course you don't know her as well

124

as I do. She would never lie."

"Perhaps not. But the ticket is as lost as the old man."

"It is an added reason to find him."

"Maybe it is the ticket I should go for. Possession of a ticket constitutes ownership."

"I confess that is the thought that brought me here. I don't think you would risk trying to cash the ticket."

"Don't underestimate me."

Fred did not seem to know what to make of this response. He decided to put it in escrow. "I have some information that may be helpful in your investigation."

"Every little bit helps. Your niece did not want me to examine the premises, out of fear of your wife."

"My wife." He said it with resignation. "Will what I say to you be confidential?"

"Like the confessional."

"I am not Catholic."

"Neither am I. Just an analogy. Nothing you say will go beyond this room." Mrs. Barnacle had ostentatiously closed the door, but would have activated the recording equipment so that there would be no need to remember what transpired.

"My wife received a phone call saying Grandpa was alright." He paused. "Or said she did."

"You doubt it?"

"What do you make of the message she was given?"

"It doesn't make any sense."

"If there was a call, I don't think that was the complete message."

"What else do you think there could have been, a ransom demand?"

"No. She would have mentioned that."

"What wouldn't she have mentioned?" This was proving to be interesting. "Go on."

"Let me take a seeming detour."

For ten minutes, Fred told the story of the amazing gas can, that came and went from the family garage. But it was his wife's reaction that was the nub of the narrative.

"She has become frantic. Hysterical. Have you ever read *Macbeth*?"

"You have?"

"Guilt is a marvelous thing. I didn't think Edna capable of it, but there is no other explanation of her behavior. I believe she knows more about the disappearance of Grandpa than she has told."

"You think she took him somewhere and left him?"

"I don't know. But it's possible."

"What do you suggest?"

"I've brought the gas can with me."

Fred looked across the table, waiting, and Norman nodded. "It seems to be all we have."

Pondering the cast of characters in this minor drama, Norman Earwick had arrived at the point Fred suggested long before he came to the office, though Fred might have been slowed by reluctance to point the finger at his wife. But it was all airy speculation. Precluded from even a discreet questioning of the neighbors, Norman had been left to his natural disinclination to do anything more than he had to. The gas can had a significance for Edna that had to be probed.

"Where does she buy her gas?" he had asked Fred.

"No special place. She looks for the lowest price."

"Self-serve?"

Fred nodded as if the phrase somehow meant more applied to Edna. "Our local service station is Updike's."

And to Updike's Norman dutifully went. Mrs. Updike

handling cash and credit cards and smoking a foot long cigarette, Mr. Updike in jeans and T-shirt and a belly that looked
as if it could use some kind of support, and in the garage two
greasy men, one with a ponytail, servicing cars. Norman got
out with the gas can while Updike filled his tank. "Did my
wife get this from you?"

Updike glanced at the can and then returned to his task.
Norman had been put on hold. When he was through,
Updike took the can and shook it. "Empty."

"I wondered if she paid a deposit on it or something."

All the wariness of one whose native land lay below sea
level crowded into Updike's eyes as he looked at Norman
from beneath unbarbered brows. He examined the can. "I
doubt it's mine."

"How so?"

"We lend them, that's all. No deposit. She paid a deposit,
it wasn't here. Also, it's in too good shape."

"Is there any way to tell where such a can came from?"

"Sure."

"How?"

A sly smile crept across Updike's face. "Keep the sales
slip."

Having made Updike's day, Norman went on to phase
two. Whatever the origin of the gas can and Edna's involve-
ment in that, there were the comings and goings of the can.
Poltergeists aside, someone had to be doing the moving. It
wasn't Edna, taking Fred's estimate of her, it wasn't Lucy.
Fred would not have brought the can to Norman if he was the
one playing games. The possibility that Grandpa had been
suddenly cured and was devoting himself to driving his old
nemesis mad was attractive, but had to be classified with the
poltergeists. Leaving Nick, the boyfriend.

5

Alex Schuler discovered only by chance that Norman Earwick had been hired by Lucy. Norman Earwick! He would never have recommended Earwick, there was something fundamentally dishonest about the man. But his advice had not been sought. Lucy, in her hour of need, had ignored the one person who had her unequivocal good disinterestedly at heart. The fact that he had been in Chicago taking depositions suddenly struck Alex as callous and indifferent. My God, Grandpa was missing, a helpless Alzheimer's patient had wandered off, a man Alex had every reason to consider close as family, and he had gone off to take depositions in Chicago. He could have sent someone, for heaven's sake, but he had always been unwilling to delegate what he could do himself. He had put routine ahead of Lucy.

"Anyone seen Norman?" Alex heard asked in the café off the entry hall of the courthouse.

"Not much since he moved to the suburbs."

"He's on the trail of a missing person."

Alex stopped his coffee an inch from his lips. Finally he had to ask the question. "I wonder who?"

"You missing someone Alex?"

"Why would someone hire Norman to do what the police can do at least as ineffectively?"

Laughter all around, but the exchange made Alex uneasy.

He could not call Lucy and ask her. It seemed vaguely unethical, a species of ambulance chasing, but of course he did not think of Lucy as a client. He called Fred.

"What's this about Norman Earwick?"

"So Lucy told you."

"I haven't talked to Norman himself yet. Doubtless hard at work."

"Maybe that gas can got him going at last."

"Gas can?"

"Didn't Lucy tell you?" Something in Fred's tone suggested he would love to. And he did, in great detail.

"And you turned it over to Norman."

"It seemed a good idea. Edna wanted me to throw it away, but it had always come back before."

Surely Fred could not be unaware that he had delivered his wife over to the suspicion of Norman Earwick.

In any case, it was true. The client he regarded as something other than a client, almost as his daughter, had bypassed him and engaged one of the sleaziest members of the sleazy band of private investigators. Their ranks were regularly replenished by bill collectors and process servers who wanted to take a step up, or work for themselves. Someone paid to deal ruthlessly with a designated foe is unlikely to readopt the Sermon on the Mount when dealing with his client. Alex was surprised by the recent fascination with the legal profession on television, in the movies, in red-hot novels that seemed to be read everywhere. But law is a dull business, with few dramatic moments, and anyone who considered the dodges and half-truths of a trial as drama should go watch one at his local courthouse. Private investigators have enjoyed a far longer run in the popular culture, and a less promising group could scarcely be imagined. And it was to this group that Norman Earwick belonged.

What to do about it? Could he, should he, do anything about it?

"How does she intend to pay him?" he asked Fred.

"With her lottery winnings."

He seemed serious. "Earwick accepted that?"

"Alex, Grandpa had a winning Power Ball ticket in his pocket."

"What's it worth?"

"The whole bundle, fifty-six million dollars."

Alex nearly dropped the phone. The thought of any significant amount of money being within the reach of Earwick was upsetting, but *this* amount!

"How do you know it's the winning ticket?"

"Lucy wrote down the numbers."

They went through it all then, and Alex listened with Norman's ears. There was no way in the world the private investigator would buy such a pig in a poke. He must realize that Lucy had resources to draw on to pay his apparently unstated fee. Still, Alex did not blame Lucy for falling into the hands of such a predator. He blamed himself. He should have been devoting himself exclusively to Lucy since the disappearance of Grandpa.

If he knew a trustworthy investigator he would hire him to monitor Earwick. Talk to Earwick? Of course. He had his girl call Norman's girl and ask if the investigator could stop by.

"He'll call back."

"Wasn't in?"

"She didn't say."

"Did she say when he might call?"

"Is it urgent?"

"No. But I want to see him."

"I'll call again."

"Good."

Norman's counter offer, brought by Alex's secretary, was that Alex stop by and see him.

"I want to talk to him."

"He's still on the phone."

Alex snatched up his phone but spoke calmly. "I hadn't thought you would be so indifferent to new business, Earwick."

"New business?"

"What else?"

"I assumed the family would have kept you abreast of developments."

Alex had always thought that grinding one's teeth was a cartoon invention, but his reaction to Earwick's smug response proved otherwise.

"You are still their lawyer." Had Lucy told him that? Was that cause for elation or dismay?

"Have you made any progress?"

"You are asking professionally?"

"Earwick, I am Lucy's lawyer. I knew her father and her mother. I know the man who has wandered off. My question is both professional and personal."

"I am following up a very concrete clue."

"The gas can."

"The gas can. No station in the vicinity provided it and the discount self serves don't get into leasing gas cans."

"Can it be traced any other way?"

"Such as?"

"The manufacturer."

"You would make a good investigator, Alex."

"I am more interested in you being a good one. And I will represent Lucy in the matter of fees."

"I send you the bills?"

"Exactly. Did she sign an agreement with you? I will want

131

a copy of that. Your secretary can call for the fax number here."

"It's good to have this added assurance that I do not labor in vain."

"You would not want to rely on the lottery."

"Ho ho."

He went out to the house to talk with Lucy but she was not there. Edna looked like the wrath of God.

"There has been another phone call."

"What did they say?"

Edna looked at him, then looked away. "A lot of non-sense."

"Edna, tell me. And you must tell the police."

"It was that same woman. She said Grandpa's all right but he misses Lucy. That's all."

"She mentioned Lucy?"

Edna nodded.

Whoever the caller was, she knew Grandpa was missing when almost no one else did. The neighbors had shown no curiosity but then they seldom saw Grandpa. Whether the person knew where Grandpa was or not, she knew the family and seemed intent on disturbing Edna.

"Has anyone else answered such a call?"

"I am not imagining them!"

"I never suggested that you were." Obviously Edna was giving way under the pressure of Grandpa's absence. Given her treatment of the old man, that was surprising, to say the least. "Would you like me to call Missing Persons? They should be told immediately."

"Missing Persons? They're missing persons, all right."

Alex took that as acquiescence and put through a call to Noonan. He turned it over to Edna so she could tell him what the caller had said.

"A lot of good that will do," Edna said when she was through.

"You never know. If he weren't with someone, he would have been found by now, Edna. And not alive."

She put a hand over her mouth and looked at him with rounded eyes.

"Do you know Lucy's class schedule?"

"It may be on her desk."

It was pinned to a corkboard over the desk in her room. Alex could imagine her studying here, a lovely young woman living in such strange circumstances. Her grandfather senile, an aunt and uncle who had more or less taken over the house, both parents gone. The sadness he felt was compounded by the sense of having failed Lucy in these past few days.

Trying to find her on campus seemed unwise, so Alex told Edna he would come by later that day. "I'll bring a pizza, all right?"

"With anchovies?"

Lucy was not there when he arrived with the pizza, Fred was not there, Edna was there, not much more cheerful than earlier, though the aroma of the pizza perked her up.

"We might just as well start. Fred won't be home for hours." Edna got beer from the refrigerator, and put out plates, her eyes never leaving the pizza.

"What time does Lucy get home?"

"I'm surprised she isn't here now." Whereupon Edna laid into the pizza. How had they been eating since Grandpa left? Edna seemed half starved. Maybe Lucy had stopped off somewhere to eat.

"She'll be with Nick."

"Of course."

Alex ate one slice of the pizza and nibbled on another. There seemed no reason to stay.

"Would you have Lucy call me when she gets home?"

Edna nodded, her mouth full of pizza. Alex bet she could put away the whole thing.

Lucy did not call that night. The next morning, early, the telephone rang. It was Fred.

"Alex, do you know where Lucy is?"

"Isn't she home?"

"That's why I'm calling. She didn't come home last night and . . ."

"I'll be right there."

At the house Lucy's room looked the way it had the previous afternoon. The bed had not been slept in. Edna could not see that any of her clothes were missing. The three of them stood there, in silence, staring at different objects in the room, all having the same thought.

6

When Rosa saw the report of the strange disappearance of Lucy Yates she felt a twinge of remorse, but she quickly deflected any blame toward Edna, for whom over the past few days she had conceived an unshakable hatred. That Lucy's disappearance was connected with Grandpa's there could be no doubt. For the first time, Grandpa's disappearance, nearly a week old, was given the attention it deserved. It was no small part of Rosa's resolve to exact condign punishment from Edna because the man she had abandoned in the parking lot of the mall in West Toledo seemed to have been abandoned by the world as well. His disappearance deserved better than to have the waters of forgetfulness close over him so completely.

"Well, I suppose you've abandoned them, in a way."

Grandpa seemed to like her, he particularly liked it when she talked to him. She continued to bring him into her workroom, not wanting to leave him alone, no matter that he did not seem to mind. But it bothered her, so into the workroom he came. He was no distraction as she wrote and watched her, wearing his single expression of bewilderment. She resolved to buy some books on Alzheimer's and read up on it, but in the meantime she was playing it by ear. In the back of her mind a story was forming that would involve a murderer with Alzheimer's. She had learned little enough from having Grandpa with her. She found it was best to treat him as a child. She certainly would not risk telling him that something had happened to Lucy.

Nell Wickers, a fervent fan and inveterate sender of e-mail had a night job at the airport parking lot, the better to keep her days for writing. Nell's complaints about customers were a staple of her messages, Rosa having commented favorably on an earlier anecdote as the possible germ of a story. That had concerned the customer who came to the pay booth to borrow the portable battery to start a frozen car. He never returned it. How had he gotten it out of the lot? Nell's theory was that he had heaved it into his trunk and gone through the pay gate without mentioning it. The question was not how he did it, but why. Rosa, remembering that, sent Nell an e-mail asking what they did if someone's parked car was out of gas. The reply was interesting. They had several cans of gas safely stored that enabled stranded motorists to start their cars. Nell went on and on about the lady who had not returned a gas can. Rosa got on the telephone to Nell.

"I hope I'm not interrupting your writing."

"*My* writing! What a surprise."

"About the woman who didn't return the gas can. How long had she been parked?"

"A couple hours. Maybe three."

"Isn't that unusual?"

"It sure is. Someone flying out, leaves a car for days. If you're just seeing someone off, you can park in short term."

"Was she driving a silvery car?" Rosa asked.

"Oh no this was a drab sedan. An Olds."

"Nell, this interests me. Will you release story rights on this to me? I'll make an acknowledgment if I actually write it."

"Of course."

"So let's explore it a bit. Describe the woman for me."

"A witch. A sour puss. When she promised to bring the can back full I knew she was lying."

"Make-up?" Rosa asked.

"How did you know?"

"Know what?"

"Her lipstick was blood red and smeared all over her mouth."

That could be Edna but the car Rosa had seen her drop Grandpa from was silver colored, a Camry. It was the fact that Edna had left her car for three hours in the airport lot that was suggestive.

"Nell, do you know anyone at the rental car counters?"

"Only my sister. She's the one who told me about this job."

"Could she find out who rented a car during the period that car was parked in your lot?"

"She'll be able to when I tell her who it's for."

"No, no, no. Then the deal's off. My name must not be mentioned."

"All right," Nell said, a little taken aback.

"Tell them you're checking something for a story you're writing."

Rosa did not believe in long shots in her stories, but real life was something else again. Nell's reply came by e-mail since Rosa did not give out her number, especially to fans. "The only woman who rented a car during those hours was young, definitely not the witch. The clerk on duty had no recollection of the transaction but the form reads Lucy Yates. She did rent a silver Camry." Rosa stopped herself from replying immediately with her thanks; she didn't want Nell to know what she had come up with. Meanwhile she pondered this interesting information.

Was Lucy in it with her aunt? But she couldn't be. At the

time the car was rented, Lucy was in Toledo in the back row of the auditorium while Rosa spoke. The rental was a mystery but Rosa felt that she had solved the main mystery. It was Edna at the wheel of the car from which Grandpa had been let out into the parking lot in West Toledo. It was time to play cat to Edna the mouse.

Rosa's four-wheeler had opaque tinted glass, so she had no hesitation in driving about with Grandpa. She strapped him in and drove to the house where he lived and cruised the street. In the driveway was the Olds that Nell had described. On her cellular phone, Rosa put through her first call to Edna. It was gratifying to hear the panic in the woman's voice as she hung up.

The following day the drama with the gas can began. Parked up the street, Rosa saw Edna put out the garbage. An hour later, she saw Lucy remove the gas can from a plastic bag and take it back to the garage. If Grandpa noticed the women he gave no sign of recognition. When Edna backed out of the driveway, Rosa followed and watched her pitch the can into a dumpster at a nearby shopping area. Rosa had stopped where she would get a good look at Edna and there was a look of satisfaction on the woman's face as she drove away. Rosa retrieved the gas can.

She checked with Nick, reminding him that he was going to show her the feature he was writing on her.

"Absolutely. It's coming along fine."

"Does your girl friend like it?"

"She thinks it's the best thing I've ever done."

"It helps to have an objective opinion."

Nick laughed. But not for long. "She's going through hell. I told you about her grandfather?"

"Is he still lost?"

"Her aunt is taking it worse than Lucy."

"How so?"

Rosa enjoyed hearing how her campaign was working. She put through another cellular call to the house and increased the pressure on Edna. Whom the gods would destroy, they first drive mad. It was time to consider how the gods would destroy Edna.

The disappearance of Lucy was unexpected and proof real life could not be controlled like a fictional plot. Rosa now was herself at the mercy of events.

7

Norman admired the four-wheeler parked on the opposite side of the street and was startled when it drove away. It was eerie, as if an empty vehicle had decided to go for a spin. Norm hated tinted glass, though his own car was equipped with it. Imagine if he had been keeping the four-wheeler rather than the house under surveillance. He was relieved to see the four-wheeler there on another occasion. That meant it belonged in the neighborhood.

Whenever Lucy left, Norm followed. Fred's bringing the gas can suggested that he should keep an eye on Edna, and that had been his original plan, but the woman had become a recluse, terrified of receiving another phone call but even more terrified not to be there if one came.

For what it was worth, probably nothing, Norm became privy to his client's life. He followed her to campus, and then went on to his office. He saw her with the boyfriend, Nick, who drove a car that was a few years shy of being a collector's item. One afternoon, Nick's car pulled into the driveway and Norm watched Lucy dash from the house and jump in. Something in her manner caused Norm to follow. He began to have second thoughts when they got on the interstate, remembering that Nick lived in Toledo. But they didn't go all the way to Toledo. Twenty miles from the city, Nick took an exit. When they reached the cross road, Norm was right behind them, visible through his untinted windshield if either of them looked, as Nick could have done through his rear-view mirror only he seemed not to have one. They took a right, not into a service station as Norm had expected but to a motel offering very attractive rates. Well, well. Nick went into the office, Lucy remaining in the car. Five minutes later, he was out, behind the wheel and driving around the building. Lucy was carrying only her purse as they unlocked the door of a unit reached directly from the space in which Nick had parked. It would have been prurient to remain, so Norm remained. What he had not expected was Nick to come out in ten minutes, hop in his car and take off. When he took the interstate entrance to Toledo, Norm took the overpass and headed back to Fort Elbow.

An investigation turns up all kinds of interesting if irrelevant things.

The following morning he was awakened by a call from Alex Schuler.

"I have a job for you."

"Well, I don't know."

"Your client is missing. Lucy Yates. She did not come home last night and her family fears the worst. They have reported it to Missing Persons."

Norman snorted.

"Exactly. Will you see if you can find her?"

"I will find her," Norman promised, and was gratified to hear the relief in the lawyer's voice.

Is this how things looked to God, he wondered. Watching people scramble around in the dark, most things a mystery to them, while all along you saw it clear as a bell? Such theological speculation was rare in Earwick who would have called himself an agnostic, if that meant covering your bets. But then it came home to him that he was not God. What if Lucy had checked out of that motel off the interstate?

She hadn't. Norman resumed his theistic reveries. It was important to have anxiety at a high pitch before he delivered the goods. There was no hesitation now about his going to the house. Noonan had not yet put in an appearance and this made Norman seem a bundle of efficiency. He checked out the house, he tried to talk to Edna, but the woman was apparently on something.

"She took an extra dose of sleeping pills last night," Fred explained.

"Was she the last one to see Lucy?"

"Don't put it that way to her."

Nick showed up and gave a good imitation of the frantic lover.

"When did you last see her?" Norman asked him.

"We had a coffee on campus in the early afternoon. I still had another class. I thought she had gone home."

The rascal. He must see what the disappearance of Lucy was doing to her uncle and aunt. Norm felt a grudging admiration for him, as Zeus might for a minor god. Nick almost overplayed his hand.

"I don't think she's in any danger."

"Why not?"

"I thought she was kidding, but she was so disappointed in the time it was taking to find Grandpa that she said she had half a mind to find out for herself if a person could just disappear without a trace."

The little vixen. Well, that meant she was stuck where she was. Nonetheless, godlike, Norm took the precaution of following Nick when he left the house. He headed on a beeline for the motel. He pulled into the space, the door opened and Lucy wearing dark glasses came out and clambered into the car.

The next motel was twelve miles further on. Norm watched them go into another ground-floor unit in the back and waited for Nick to leave. He had decided it was too risky to let this run on longer. She might transfer to another motel without his knowledge and where would his omniscience be then?

He went around to the office and asked to see the manager. The large woman with overbite said she was the manager. Norman showed her his identification.

"Oh my God."

"Don't blow my cover."

"What is it?"

"I am going to pick up a runaway who is occupying 124."

"124. 124." Inez searched the registration cards. "But there is a Nicholas Earwick in that unit."

Nicholas Earwick? Well, that would have to be kept quiet. Inez was begging him to keep the name of the motel out of it. He explained to her that she had an unmarried couple registered in her motel.

"You're lucky she's not a minor."

"Oh my God."

"Don't blaspheme."

"I'm sorry."

"I make formal notification to you that I am about to take her into custody. Here is my card."

"Earwick," she cried. "Is he a relative?"

"No, my dear. Like you, he has taken my name in vain."

He had her come along, as witness, and also because she could open the door if Lucy did not. But Lucy opened at the second insistent knocking. When she looked over the safety chain and saw Norman, her face lit up with a smile.

"That proves it," she cried.

Norm got her out of there, not liking how this scene would

be narrated by Inez when she was questioned.

"It has been thirty-four hours since I was reported missing. Not bad."

Norman acknowledged her praise.

"So why haven't you found Grandpa yet? It's going into the second week!"

As Nick had said, acting as if he were just remembering a conversation, Lucy had meant to make chumps out of Missing Persons by disappearing without a trace and then surfacing, showing how hopelessly inept they were. On the other hand, if they located her, she could taunt them as she was taunting Norman about not yet having found her grandfather.

"Missing Persons would never have found you."

"I believe it. How did you?"

"Trade secret."

"You ought to sell it to Lieutenant Noonan."

"He couldn't afford it."

"When you retire then."

"Hey, I'm a young man." He pushed his chin out so the slack wasn't so obvious.

The return of the prodigal Lucy brought joy and hope to the house. Even Edna brightened up, putting on another coat of lipstick that made her look like Mrs. Dracula after a night out. The media were alerted and soon the street was full of mobile units, raising their antenna and crews showing off on the lawn.

Lucy told the world of what she had done and why. Not, she graciously added, that it took anything away from the professional skill of Norman Earwick. Norman made a cameo appearance and then it was time for Grandpa. Newsmen and newswomen spoke in grave tones about the earlier unreported tragedy that had struck this family which was the basis for the daring experiment conducted by Lucy Yates.

"Can a human being simply disappear?" asked a frowning blonde whose smile never went away. "Can a helpless old man wander away from home and disappear into thin air? That is the question posed in this city tonight."

Fred kept out of range of camera and microphone but Edna rose to the occasion.

"It has been horrible," she said. "Horrible."

Norman went off to the side of the yard for a smoke and Fred wandered over.

"How did you find her?"

"Just routine."

"Why isn't Grandpa routine?" Fred asked.

"Because someone has him. That's the meaning of those phone calls."

"But why would anyone want an elderly man with Alzheimer's? There hasn't been any demand for money."

"We live in a strange world, Fred. Say, that's a nice four-wheeler one of your neighbors has."

The vehicle had pulled away from the curb and was now threading its way among the media vans.

"No one in this neighborhood owns a car like that. Probably a journalist."

8

Edna wondered what would have become of what was left of her mind if Lucy had not been returned so soon. It was such a relief that Edna was not immediately angry with her niece for pulling such a stunt. But she was back and all the excitement of the television people made Edna think that Grandpa too would soon be found.

She lay on her bed, having told Fred she was just fine and no she didn't want anything to eat. Maybe he could send out for a pizza later? Meanwhile she wanted to lie on her bed and stare at the ceiling and not think of anything. She could hear Lucy talking with Nick and Fred, reviewing what had been happening. Nick had been in on it all along. Why didn't they marry and move out and leave her alone. Her and Fred.

If only Grandpa were found. She wanted him found dead, she admitted that to herself. Only that would cancel out those dreadful phone calls. Somehow that woman knew what she had done, she knew everything, the rental car, leaving Grandpa standing there in the parking lot. When Edna thought of that solitary figure standing helpless and alone at night in a strange place, she felt no pity at all. Sometimes she wished she had not acted as she had. Then she would not have been harassed by that caller and had all those tricks played on her with the gas can. What did the woman want?

In the last phone call, the one Edna had kept secret, the

woman had congratulated her on using her niece's name when she rented the car.

"What do you want!"

There was a long pause, in which the woman's breathing sounded in Edna's ear like the tempo of doom. She wanted to slam down the phone but she couldn't. She was mesmerized. And then the woman spoke again.

"You."

And hung up.

It was an open threat and Edna had cowered in her room. Then the disappearance of Lucy had brought terrible thoughts that the woman had taken Lucy as she had Grandpa. Did she think Lucy was herself? Was that possible? A little flicker of hope began. Lucy seemed a small sacrifice to pay for the return of peace of mind.

Edna thought of the carefree days when she had spent hours at the bridge table. She had canceled all engagements. The thought of a deck of cards did not even tempt her, that is how far gone she was. She had rejoiced when Lucy came back, that had to be said for her, but when she learned what Lucy had done, pretended to be gone, she could have brained her.

Now lying on her bed she realized that the return of Lucy had brought back her own terror. She reached for her pills and shook some into her hand, not even looking to see how many and washed them down with the stale water from the glass on her bed stand. She lay perfectly still and felt sleep coming on, wanting it but dreading as well the imagined terrors that filled her dreams.

The banging that had been splitting her head in her dreams continued when she struggled into wakefulness. Someone was at the door. Why didn't Fred answer it? But there were no sounds of voices in the house. She managed to sit up. She sat on the edge of the bed. They must have gone for pizza and forgotten to take their house key. Edna pushed herself to her feet and staggered out of her room. Why the front door? She directed herself at it, thinking this could still be a dream. She undid the chain and turned the lock and opened the door.

A short stout woman stood there.

"Who are you!" But she already knew. She tried to shut the door, but the woman grabbed her arm and pulled her into the night.

"I have come for you."

9

Who said that in history things happen a first time as tragedy, and a second time as farce? Alex wondered what the third time was supposed to be. Fred and Lucy and Nick had gone off for pizza and when they returned Edna was gone. The trio was still celebrating what they regarded as Lucy's triumph and now this.

Alex drove to the house as soon as Lucy called him. He had been intending to give her a proper scolding for what she had done and for a fleeting moment thought Edna's disappearance was another stunt. The house that had been full of hope and rejoicing just hours before while the media circus went on, was now a place of silent gloom.

"Have you notified anyone?"

Fred shook his head. "Of what? That a grown woman is not at home? It hasn't been an hour since she was here. I didn't want Lucy to call you. What do we know? It's only because of what has been happening that we are reacting this way."

Of the three, Fred seemed the coolest, and it was his wife they had found gone when they returned with the pizza. She had been asleep when they left, Fred thought she might have taken sleeping pills. But when they came back, she was gone.

"No signs of a struggle?"

"She left the front door open," Fred said.

"Could she be walking in her sleep?"

"In her current condition, who knows?"

"Her car is here?"

"Yes."

"Have you looked for her?" Alex asked.

It seemed they had decided to eat the pizza first. Lucy was the one who decided that Edna had gone the way of Grandpa. Because of the phone calls she had received.

"Were they threatening?"

"She certainly thought so."

Lucy said, "I think we should search the neighborhood."

For the next several hours, Lucy and Nick on foot, Fred and Alex in different cars, they went over a twelve-block area with a fine tooth comb. There was no sign of Edna.

Back at the house, Alex chaired the conference they held.

"First, I recommend that we do not inform the police or the media just yet."

"Why?"

"Peter and the Wolf."

"How about Norman Earwick?"

"No! Chances are that she is going to come back tonight. Look, she could be at a movie."

"She's more likely to find a bridge game."

"Where did she play?"

Lucy knew and she went off to call and ask if Edna was there.

"How would she have gotten there?" Fred asked.

"She could take a cab."

"Alex, her purse is in her room, by her bed."

That was when Alex really began to take this seriously. But he could imagine the reaction at Missing Persons if they enlisted their help a third time. The media would be even more inclined to be skeptical. All the sympathy they had shown the family at the happy return of Lucy would swiftly change into hostility. They would feel they had been duped.

"So are we agreed? We keep a vigil and hope and pray that she walks in that door."

Alex himself stayed until two in the morning. Fred sat in the middle of the living room couch, vowing to stay up all night. Nick said he couldn't leave without knowing what was going on. He was given Grandpa's room. Alex was almost glad to get out of there.

Edna did not return that night. Two days later, Alex volunteered to look at the body of a woman that had been fished out of the river, when it had drifted ashore. At the morgue, Hogan pulled out a drawer and there was Edna, dead as could be.

Part Four

SWITCH

1

Since Edna had no religious affiliation other than generic Protestant and she had never gone to church, the service was held at the mortuary, Camel's, named not in tribute to a major supplier but after the founder who had anglicized Cameau. The service was called ecumenical and designed to offend no one. Lucy was asked to pick the readings and she selected a portion of Tennyson's *In Memoriam* and Catullus's farewell to his brother. Winston Camel threw in something from Edgar Guest and Walt Whitman. All readings had organ accompaniment.

The garish little chapel was filled mostly with bridge players. In the manner of such services of late, mourners were asked to step forward and recount some especially memorable moment spent with the deceased.

Fred said with wonderful ambiguity that he would never forget the day they met. Lucy spoke with sincere sorrow of her late aunt and broke into tears that Grandpa was not here. Perhaps, she suggested, we are memorializing him today as well. Tears were general throughout the room. Nick read some pages he had written which seemed to have little to do with the occasion, a lush description of a river flowing ever to the sea, but the connection doubtless was that Edna had drowned in the Prune. A woman with a croaking voice told of the time she and Edna had made a grand slam in hearts doubled and redoubled. She smacked her dry mouth in punctuation of what she said. Then she looked out at the audience with a bright mad eye and cried, "God does not renege!" She was helped to her seat.

The cremation was done off stage and, as he had requested, the urn of ashes was then given to Fred. Why did he want them? He said he would scatter them over the river, the place she had chosen to end her life. The urn? He would keep that as a personal reminder.

And then it was over. After a certain milling about in the main entrance hall and on the walk outside, the mourners went cheerfully off to their conveyances, pushing thoughts of mortality from their minds.

Lucy, convoyed by Nick on one side and Alex on the other, went off for a commemorative breakfast. A four-wheeler with tinted glass pulled out of the lot as they went to the car and Norman Earwick got out of his. He took Fred's hand.

"I share your thoughts."

"Thank you."

"Did you see that four-wheeler?"

But the vehicle was gone and no one had taken notice of it. Norman had the good sense to decline the invitation that he join them. The search for Grandpa must go on. He was startled when Lucy burst into tears. She was hurried on to the car.

"Did I say something wrong?" he asked Fred.

"What interests you in that four-wheeler?"

"I'm thinking of getting one."

They parted.

The assumption was that Edna had done away with herself. Weighed down by grief at what had happened to Grandpa, harassed and unnerved by telephone calls and objects coming and going from the garage, this strong-willed and domineering woman had cracked. Disintegration had then been swift and total. Finally, doubtless under the influence of pills she had taken, she fled to the river and hurled herself off the bridge into the Prune River up which centuries ago French missionaries had paddled.

"The river is three miles away," Nick said.

Had he never heard of mothers who lift half-ton trucks off their stricken children, hysteria granting them superhuman strength? What are three miles to a distraught woman intent on suicide?

"But someone would have seen her."

So what? How many distraught women have you stopped to help?

In short, all objections to the possibility that Edna had risen from her bed and gone three miles on foot to throw herself in the river dissolved before the apparent actuality. If she did it, it could be done. The question thus being begged, funeral services were arranged.

For some, grief was distracted by a reporter who had decided to devote himself to discovering the winner of the still unclaimed Power Ball jackpot of nearly two weeks ago. Fifty-six million dollars awaited a young woman who had bought the ticket from a vendor whose address fortunately did not put it in the neighborhood of the Yates' home. Giving superstition full range, Lucy had bought the ticket at a fast food store called grandly Santa Lucia. The proprietor of the Santa Lucia, Klaus Wasser, added his plea that the winner come forward. Klaus would get his own reward for selling the winning ticket.

For Lucy this was one more reminder that her grandfather was still lost, still no reports on his real or possible whereabouts. The publicity when Lucy staged her own disappearance and focused attention on Grandpa, the media attention, like snowflakes on a warm window pane, all too soon was gone.

"Maybe I should tell them Grandpa has the ticket," Lucy said.

"Good God no," Fred said.

"Most inadvisable," said Alex.

"They'd be after the ticket and the hell with Grandpa," Nick said.

They breakfasted in the Hilton and the posh surroundings swiftly took their thoughts from loss. Fred had a Bloody Mary, to everyone's surprise but Lucy's. With Edna gone, beer suddenly appeared in the refrigerator and there was an array of bottles in the cupboard above the sink. Alex joined him, but Nick and Lucy settled for coffee.

"Edna and I played bridge together," Fred said. "Years ago."

"Wasn't she a black belt or something?"

"Master."

"You mean mistress."

"Now now."

Nick swerved to talk of Mark McGuire and his current home run production. "Where do you go after seventy?" he wondered.

"I hope to find out," Alex said.

"How old are you?"

"You should never ask a lawyer his age."

"I should think being older would help business," Nick said.

"I am nineteen years older than Lucy."

"Is that all?" Lucy said and Alex beamed.

Nick was counting on his fingers. "I thought you were older than that."

"He told you not to ask a lawyer his age."

"Of course I'm old enough to be her father. Her father and I were boyhood friends."

"And her mother?"

"I knew her as well."

"As long as you knew her father?" Nick asked.

"Almost."

But this reminder of Lucy's losses threatened to cast gloom over the table as thoughts of Edna did not and Nick was permitted to reintroduce the subject of baseball.

Lucy's was not a naturally meditative temperament but the events through which she had passed would have rendered a stone thoughtful. Her father's ghost had haunted her childhood, her mother taking the wedding vows a step farther and not permitting even death to sever the bond. The simple faith and generosity of her mother had been a lesson Lucy resolved to learn, and her love for Nick would ultimately be tested as an alloy or the real thing by comparison with her parents'. It was altogether typical of her mother to take Grandpa in with them when his condition deteriorated to the point that many urged his institutionalization. Lucy well remembered Edna's visits while her mother was still alive, the criticism tempered by the recognition that this solution was far less expensive. What would one more mouth mean in a household that must already provide for Lucy and her mother? The house had to be heated and cooled in any case. Edna went on and on, making it sound as if Lucy's mother were actually gaining from taking her father-in-law into her home.

The illness and swift death of her mother had given Lucy a profound sense of the fragility of life. It is the prerogative of the young to feel immortal and to regard their own aging as a process that stretches off into an indefinite distance. The death of her mother had deprived Lucy of this sense. Without being morbid, she had the realization that everything could be over at any minute, no matter how old you were.

Nor did simply growing older seem intrinsically attractive. After all, Edna had grown older and what a sour and narrow view of life she had. There was a mad logic in the fact that she had been undone by what happened to Grandpa. Lucy's mother had put the old man in her particular care, and it had often been a temptation to flare out at Edna's treatment of Grandpa. But more important than a satisfied anger was the even temper of the house. After all, was Edna's existence any more human than Grandpa's?

Grandpa. He had to be found! Lucy's effort to put new energy into the search for him had met with only mixed success.

That afternoon, she called Norman Earwick. "Has that gas can led to anything?"

2

Hazel was good about it, Fred granted her that. Even in West Toledo she had read of the woman who took a dive off the bridge into the Prune. Mrs. Frederick Huff.

"I've been married all along."

"I know."

"I should have told you."

"I mean I knew. Come on, why else did it always have to be a daytime thing. Besides, you had the look of a husband."

"What look is that?"

"Deprived."

It was the afternoon of Edna's funeral. Fred had set off with the urn of ashes in the trunk of his car, but the traffic on the bridge decided him to postpone the ceremony of dumping Edna's mortal remains into the angry water. Now that there was no impediment to it, he had to see Hazel. They had gone out to his car to talk. As she said "Deprived" she turned to him and gave him a look. The look. He lowered his head and snuggled his face in her breasts. Edna's had been like poached eggs, but only melons, shapely melons, could symbolize Hazel's. She ran her fingers through his hair.

"And you can relax, Fred. I still don't want to marry again."

She checked out early, leaving things in the hands of the kind of kid you can get to work in fast food franchises, and

161

they drove to her apartment where they disported themselves like kids. It was the way it had been in the beginning. Now that he thought of it, Fred considered it an insult that Edna had never even suspected him. She must have thought he was as dried up as she was. Thanks to Hazel, he knew this was not so.

"Wanna talk about it?" she asked as, spent and panting, they lay in one another's arms.

"What?"

"Her."

"No!"

"You know how I imagined her?"

"How?"

"A short fat woman with the face of a bulldog."

"She was tall. Why did you think she was short?"

"Oh, I thought I saw her several times when we were together."

"A short fat woman?"

"Obviously I was mistaken. Probably my conscience. I used to imagine the angry wife descending on us. We never were discreet, you know."

"She hadn't the least idea."

"You'll have to explain that to me some time. I thought I had left my mark upon you." She was twisting the hair on his chest into curls.

"Edna hated that."

"What?"

"The hair on my chest."

"Jealous?"

He tweaked her nipple and passion took possession of them once more. After that, they sat in the living room and drank wine coolers.

"Was the funeral awful?"

He described it for her. "I have her ashes in the trunk."

"Fred, you don't."

"I am going to spill them into the river."

Hazel decided that was poetic. She would like to see it done.

"It's like scattering your past to the four winds. So what does Fred do now?"

"Probably move back to Toledo. But not until we find Grandpa."

"There are so many old people at the mall who are probably as bad off as he is. The woman I thought was your wife walks one around from time to time. Not regular, like so many of them."

"Short and fat."

"Face like a bull dog."

"That's not Edna. Not just the looks. She would never have taken the trouble to go for a walk with Grandpa."

3

The night Edna had left the house, before the body was found, Alex Schuler had already rejected the notion that the woman, maddened by the pressure of recent events, had fled three miles in order to hurl herself into the Prune. If suicide had been her aim, she had the means in the bottle beside her bed, a far less repellant exit ticket than plummeting from a bridge. Nor did it make much sense that she had left the front door open. But if not suicide, then murder, and who?

It had become more and more difficult to take seriously Edna's claim that she was receiving harassing and threatening phone calls. Obviously she was feeling guilty about the fact that Grandpa had disappeared on her watch and the subsequent pressure unglued her. However unaccustomed Edna had been to blaming herself, once she got the hang of it, she overdid it. But not to the point that she would have killed herself.

She had taken some sleeping pills, and that meant she had been awakened. Had someone gotten into the house, pulled her from her bed, hustled her out the front door and on to the river where they pitched her over the railing? Something like that was infinitely more plausible than suicide, but not very plausible taken in itself.

Edna had no friends, but she had no real enemies either. Bridge players respected her skill, and in the abstract atmo-

164

sphere of a bridge club, skill was all that mattered. No one who knew her could like her, but there had been no active animosity. In order for there to have been a murder, there had to be a murderer, and a murderer unless he was nuts needed a motive. But who profited or benefited from Edna's demise? Fred, of course.

Alex had watched Fred during the breakfast at the Hilton. He was not your usual bereaved husband. He could be forgiven for feeling that a great weight had been taken from him. Had he himself removed that weight?

The problem with that was that Fred had come back to the house with Lucy and Nick. The fact that they had gone in separate cars to the pizza parlor provided no wedge; they had met at the parlor and returned home together. But Alex remembered Nick's comment on that.

"Funny. He beat us home and we had the pizza."

Alex sat back and imagined Fred dashing into the house, picking up Edna from her bed, taking her out the front way and putting her still asleep in his car. Later, unobserved, he drives off to the river and threw her overboard. Logically possible? Who could say? But Alex rejected the thought as unworthy of what he knew of Fred. A more longsuffering husband Alex had yet to meet. Edna's treatment of him gave celibacy unsuspected allure.

It had to be the mysterious phone caller.

Norman Earwick was unreceptive to such speculation. "Alex, the indifference of the police to her death is total. As far as they are concerned, she was some nutty dame who decided to throw herself in the river. Given the way that family has been registering on the police radar lately, they may even wonder if she *had* to be nuts to want out of there."

"They sent out a crew to inspect the scene."

"Don't hold your breath."

"They dusted for fingerprints."

"Fingerprints are archaic."

"I still have mine."

"But can you prove they are yours beyond a reasonable doubt?"

"Norman, someone killed that woman."

"You mean someone else?"

"You know what I mean. Now, she was receiving phone calls . . ."

"Alex, no one else ever got such a phone call. The caller only calls when Edna is there. How does she know? Chalk it up to hallucinations, Alex. She felt guilty because of the way she treated the old man. He remains my only objective. And I am going to find him."

"If only you could have the same luck with him you had with Lucy."

"Luck?"

Later Alex learned that Captain Manfredi had taken over the investigation of Edna Huff's death, bumping Noonan off the case.

Several days after the funeral, Alex had Lucy in for an avuncular talk. It seemed a good time to review her financial situation. He left the papers on his desk, and took Lucy to matching chairs in a corner of the office for a less formal setting. How beautiful she was. The anxieties of recent weeks had given a new dimension to her beauty, her character illuminating the outer surface and rendering it even more attractive. Her love of and devotion to her grandfather were a continuation of her feelings for her mother and for her father. Alex had not failed to notice Lucy's surprise at their relative ages, nor did the remark that he was old enough to be her father have any negative effect. Nick was a good boy but such a boy, shallow, without experience. Next to Lucy, he seemed a child. Old hopes stirred in Alex's breast, hopes that his life could receive a final endorsement when the daughter of his old friends became his wife. But only a mind reader could have guessed that these were his thoughts as he got Lucy settled.

"It has been some time since we had a talk."

"And meanwhile I have disappointed you."

"How so?"

"Hiring that detective. Pretending to be lost."

Alex waved away these peccadilloes. "They were indications of your love and concern for Grandpa."

"A fat lot of good they did."

"Earwick is going at the job with renewed energy."

Lucy's expression told what she thought that was worth.

"I want you to tell me again about the lottery ticket. You have seen these stories in the paper."

She nodded.

"You are the young woman described."

"That's right. I don't dare stop at the Santa Lucia now." She leaned forward. "Are we ready to use that ticket?"

"Use it?"

"Imagine if people knew that Grandpa is carrying around a ticket worth fifty-six million dollars. Their reward . . ."

"Lucy, there would be too many who would want the whole amount. No, that ticket would only mean more danger for Grandpa, if . . ."

"If he is still alive."

"If he is still alive. I am glad you realize we have to accept that he may not be."

"Only in my mind. Here." She touched her breast. "Here, I know he is alive and that woman who called is taking care of him. The first thing she said to Edna was that Grandpa was okay."

Edna had not been far gone when she reported the first call, so her mental imbalance was the result not the cause of the calls. But whether she was benevolent or malevolent would tell the story. As for why anyone would take possession of Grandpa, Alex just gave up. His profession depended on the rational connection between events, cause and effect, the antecedent bringing about the consequent. Above all, what human beings did demanded a why, the aim or purpose of the act. Of course, in court the defendant's lawyer would chip away at the fundamental assumption of law, suggesting that forces over which his client had no control explained the action—upbringing, a chemical imbalance in the brain, psychosis. But these too were explainers, however much they were meant to exonerate a defendant. Cause and effect still reigned supreme. But in the case of Grandpa's disappearance, that damned gas can, the phone calls, Edna's death, Alex frankly gave up.

"We will leave it in the capable hands of Norman Earwick."

"I thought you considered him crooked."

"That is an essential requirement for success in what he does."

"You think he's after the lottery ticket, don't you?"

"Yes. But Grandpa has the lottery ticket, doesn't he?"

"Unless someone took it from his pocket."

And they observed a moment's silence, during which they wondered if the woman who called had gone through Grandpa's pockets. Of course she would have, to find out who he was. But who would think to check the hankie pocket in his corduroy coat?

4

The random was assuming a pattern, and the spider spinning it was the driver of the four-wheeler with tinted windows. Norman had first noticed the vehicle because it was of a kind he genuinely would like to own, though he did not think its suburbanite aura quite went with his professional persona.

"It's too young for you," Mrs. Barnacle said.

"That isn't what I meant."

"Well, it's what I meant. People our age . . ."

Norman cut her off. Our age! Mrs. Barnacle was middle-aged and was getting a little too chummy for his taste.

"What do you know of James Joyce?" he demanded.

"Besides the *Portrait*, not much."

"That's good." What the hell was she talking about it? He would look up Joyce on the web. When he did, typing Joyce and letting Yahoo do the looking, he got a steamy page from Joyce Orange who wanted to sell him some revealing photographs of herself. Thus distracted, he forgot what he was after. He clicked away from the page when Mrs. Barnacle came into his office and dropped a sheet of paper on his desk.

"That's the registration on the tag. She's Rosa Charrin."

Norman picked up the sheet and saw that the four-wheeler was registered in the name of Rosa Subiaco Inc.

"It says Subiaco."

"That's her real name. Charrin is a pen name."

"What does she need a pen name for?"

"She's an author, a writer. She has written a ton of books."

"Yeah?"

"You can check this on the web, but she is one of the most prolific authors now active."

"Writes a lot, does she?"

"Go to the library. There are shelves devoted to her, of course they have to buy multiple copies of her stuff."

"What kind of money does that bring in?"

"Piles."

Well, well. Norman thanked Mrs. Barnacle with a distracted air. It was time to start putting things together.

Item. Norman, when checking out things at the Huff residence, notices four-wheeler for the first time, and admires it.

Item. Fred tells him that no one in the neighborhood owns such a vehicle.

Item. While keeping the house under surveillance, he notices that the four-wheeler is often similarly parked. Were they both there for the same reason?

Item. The presence of the vehicle made it possible that she—he knew the driver was a she now—was responsible for the coming and going of the gas can.

Item. The vehicle had been there during the hullabaloo after his recovery of Lucy, he had gone in pursuit, but she had eluded him. Rephrase that, she could not know she was being followed. The traffic had swallowed her up.

Item. She was at the funeral.

Putting these things together. Because of the gas can, the driver of the four-wheeler and the one who phoned Edna were one and the same person. That made it likely that she had Grandpa. Furthermore, her target was clearly Edna, for whatever reason. Finally, Norman concluded that she had snatched Edna and dumped her into the Prune. With all that, who needed motive?

Now came the big question. Had Rosa whoever found the lottery ticket? Did she know that beside a gaga old man, she had a ticket worth fifty-six million dollars? Mrs. Barnacle said the woman made a pile as a writer, but whatever she made that amount would catch her attention. Maybe that had been the reason for the snatch in the first place.

Norman rocked back and forth, humming. How about this? That ticket was a family ticket, at least one that included Edna. Lucy in cahoots with Rosa Subiaco, removes Grandpa and the ticket, thereby causing consternation in Edna. Edna threatens to sue them if they try to ace her out of the winnings, whereupon . . .

But Norman had begun to shake his head halfway through that hypothesis. It depended on their knowing they had the winning ticket before the drawing. So the hell with reasons. The real issue was how he was going to get hold of that ticket—and Grandpa too, if he could arrange it.

The address on the registration form went against Rosa making the big bucks Mrs. Barnacle said she did. It was a crummy neighborhood, on the edge of another old neighborhood that had been taken over by yuppies and brought back to its alleged original glory. Norman had never felt any urge to own a house, let alone an ancient one that would soak up money like a sponge, and why? So you could pretend you were living seventy-five or a hundred years ago. At least Rosa wasn't that kind of nut.

Time to check out the place. Before he got into his Trans Am, Norman stood looking at it. Once the last word, it no doubt about it had a dated look. He was hanging on to the past the way those Yuppies were trying to recover it. By God, he would price a four-wheeler. He liked the thought of sitting high above the traffic, in a vehicle that would instill fear in the hearts of other motorists.

His engine sounded fluttery when he started it and when he drove out of the lot there was a complaint from his shocks. He had been driving a clunker for months without recognizing it.

He found the neighborhood and the house and a surprise. If that wasn't Nick's car parked in front of the house, Norman was a monkey's uncle, which he wasn't. Nephew, maybe.

He drove right on by, trying to figure out what this meant. Was Nick in a conspiracy against Lucy and her Grandpa? He would have liked to park and await events, but his car was known to Nick and if he was up to something he would certainly keep an eye out for anything threatening. Norman didn't even take a U-turn and pass the house the other way. Was Grandpa in there? Was the lottery ticket?

Norman did what a man can do in a tight situation. He drove to Applebee's and sitting at the bar ordered a double bourbon. It was a funny place, but the drinks were generous and there were television sets all over the place to drive out thought. And, of course, the waitresses.

5

A case could be made for human sacrifice, Rosa told herself. As a form of expiation, it had no equal. Edna balanced off the man before Julius. One more victim and Rosa would be square with the order of the cosmos. Not that she had any definite candidate in mind, but Nick's mention of the private investigator Lucy had hired to find Grandpa intrigued her.

"Is he any good?"

"He found Lucy just like that, and we took precautions. That was impressive."

Hmm. It would not do to have some mercenary draw attention to her. Such a person would not fret about search warrants, but just break in and once Grandpa was found, Rosa would have some explaining to do. And curiosity about her mode of living could lead to more than embarrassment if the past came under scrutiny. She encouraged Nick to keep her up on things.

What an invaluable and naive young man he was. He was her unwitting spy in the enemy camp. How often had he sat talking to her here and never guessed that the ostensible object of the great manhunt was under the same roof. As a precaution, she took Grandpa downstairs to the quarters Julius had occupied. There was no sense in taking unnecessary chances, even with Nick.

The only car Nick knew she had was the battered Fiesta

out back. She kept the four-wheeler in a garage across the alley. It was the Fiesta that she drove to Earwick's office at three one morning. Information she had gleaned from the web about doors operated by magnetic cards proved accurate and she was soon seated at Earwick's desk and getting some sense of her adversary. He did not seem formidable. There was an audio system to record what went on in his office and she activated it, paused and then whispered huskily, "Rosebud." The file in Mrs. Barnacle's room told her of the clothing Lucy had brought. It was stored on an upper shelf of the closet. Rosa took it along. Grandpa could use a change.

If her nocturnal visit drew a reaction from Earwick, he did not pass it on to Lucy and thence to Nick and so not to her. But Rosa had little doubt that that whispered word the next time he activated the audio system would get his attention. Increasingly it looked as if Norman Earwick would be her next sacrificial victim.

The Aztecs were judged a cruel uncivilized people, but Rosa was sure this was due to a failure of imagination. The judgment meant little more than that practices long ago in Mexico were unlike those in present day Peoria. But the truth was that cruelty was a human characteristic. Look at the swath Coronado had cut through the southwest, destroying villages and brutally executing native Americans, all in search of gold. The Aztecs seemed to be purer of motive. Rosa liked to think they shared her own cosmology.

The world is not governed by chance. Its order, the balancing of opposites, is the source of the only moral law there is. Any deviation from the order of things requires with utmost necessity compensatory action. The ancient Greeks had thought of the world as a pie, whose quadrants were occupied by deities more familiarly known as fire, air, earth and water.

Injustice consisted in one element straying into the territory of another and this trespass had to be expiated. The trespassing resulted in a mixed body composed of elements, so every product of change was a standing injustice that could only be rectified by its dissolution or death.

There was a grim logic in this picture, and Rosa had made it her own. This is the concept that lay behind her stories, her plots, her flaming lovers. All their conquests had to be repaid with defeats. As in her books, so now in the real world Rosa had become the agent of cosmic order.

"I wish Lucy could meet you," Nick said.

"We've been through that."

His visits were explained by the fiction that he needed ever more information for his feature story. She had also agreed to look at some of his fiction.

"Stay with non-fiction," she advised.

"What's wrong with it?"

"You wouldn't want to know."

"But I do."

"It's not a story."

"Oh no."

"Do you know what I mean?"

He did. No plot. How could he have violated his own chosen theory of fiction?

"Remembering is the greater part of art."

"I like the way you consider your writing art."

"It is."

"Oh I agree."

"Many wouldn't. But they are nameless wimps now and I will still be read long after they have returned their elements to the cosmic pool."

He didn't know what to make of her boasting. Did he

think authors were humble? How could you be humble and still assume that others would be interested in what you devised upon the page? It was like buttonholing strangers and telling them all about yourself. Call it fiction, and you get paid for it.

Finally Nick told her about the lottery ticket.

"I thought his pockets were empty." She knew they were. She knew that Edna had removed every possibility of identification before abandoning Grandpa in the parking lot of the mall in West Toledo.

"You know the top pocket on a man's jacket?" He patted the appropriate spot on his tee shirt.

"Ah."

"How did Lucy know it was the winning ticket?"

"She wrote down the numbers and gave the ticket to him. They were to share."

"How much?"

"Fifty-six million dollars."

Rosa stared at him. "Say it again."

He did, with a smile, as if he himself had won that amount. "Fifty-six million dollars."

"No wonder they're so frantic to find the old man."

"Oh Lucy would gladly give up the ticket to have Grandpa back."

Such devotion troubled Rosa's feminine heart. It is painful to hear another woman praised by a male, particularly one with as many charms as Nick.

"When will you marry?"

"As soon as possible."

"When the lottery ticket is recovered?"

Nick's expression changed. "I hope Grandpa is found all right but without the ticket. Can you imagine marrying a woman with that kind of money?"

"It would bother you?"

"Of course."

"What if her writing succeeds and yours does not?"

"That would be different."

"A successful author could still attract you?"

He didn't bite. She hadn't expected him to. Still, he must at least be used to her looks now. Even at the beginning, he had given no indication that he found her repellant. Weaning him from Lucy would be a challenge she would like to accept, but first things first. The first thing of all was Norman Earwick.

The man might be incompetent, but as his discovery of Lucy showed, he could be lucky. And then she checked out the kind of car he drove and realized she had seen it before. It had been so often parked at the curb when she checked out the Huff house, that she had assumed it was a neighbor's. The thought that he must have noticed her vehicle sent a warning tremor through her short body. A private investigator could easily check out the ownership of a vehicle.

"Good news," Nick told her on the phone. "Earwick says he is sure he knows where Grandpa is being kept."

Rosa immediately went on red alert.

She stowed Grandpa in the basement, checking the hankie pocket of his corduroy jacket. The lottery ticket was there. She glanced at fifty-six million dollars' worth of cardboard and put it back in his pocket.

6

"*Citizen Kane*," Mrs. Barnacle said impatiently. "The last whispered word in that memorable movie." Was she quoting a review?

"Is that your voice?"

"No."

"So who recorded it?"

"Look, you're the private investigator."

"Never forget it."

He was hard at work, planning the tactics of his descent upon Rosa Subiaco when Mrs. Barnacle broke in.

"Those clothes Lucy brought, her grandfather's shirt and trousers, they're gone!"

He let her lead him out to the closet and look at the shelf where the clothes had been kept. He agreed that they were not there.

"You're not a cross dresser, are you?"

She closed her eyes until the pain passed. "Mr. Earwick, don't you see what this means? Someone has broken into this office. That word recorded on your taping system is a message."

By the time he got back to his desk, it was clear to him. Rosebud, hell. That was the audible signature of Rosa Subiaco, letting him know she had been on the premises. She had taken the clothes for the hell of it. This was the woman who had driven Edna nuts with a disappearing and re-appearing gas can. Norman Earwick smiled smugly. Well, she would find that she was not dealing with Edna now. If games were to be played, then by God games would be played.

He put through a call to Lucy. "I think I have located your grandfather. I hope to have him in custody safe and sound. Stand by."

He hung up. One always called his shot in pool, lest a ball seem to be pocketed accidentally. In the game he was about to play with Rosa Subiaco, he wanted to call his shot. Hence the call to Lucy.

He had to assume that Rosa knew the car he drove. He would rent a car. He drove to the airport, left his clunker in the lot and went inside the terminal to rent a car.

"You're local," the girl said, looking at his driver's permit.

"Is that unusual?"

"Oh yes. The last one I had was that poor woman who threw herself in the river a few days ago."

"You're kidding."

No, she wasn't. And she was happy to give Norman all the details. So this is how Edna had done it. When he left the terminal, a thought occurred to him, and he walked through short term parking to a pay booth.

And old lady with flared plastic glasses looked out at him warily.

"As a matter of curiosity what do you do if someone's car runs out of gas? Say, they forgot to turn off the motor in their rush to catch a plane?"

"We have gas here. But some people take advantage of it."

"Drive off with the can?"

179

"Promising they will get it refilled and bring it back. I'll never fall for that again."

"Thanks you."

"Are you out of gas?"

"Madam, I have a full tank and am raring to go."

Knowledge is power and he who has it will bring home the bacon. It helped to have the hitherto mysterious reduced to simple fact. Somehow Rosa had learned what he had learned of how Edna got rid of the old man, and she had used the unreturned gas can to shatter the woman's reason. But wait a minute. Whether or not Edna was nutty, that did not explain her death. Rosa had done that, Norman was sure of it. It added more zest to his task to realize he was about to apprehend a murderer.

He had obtained Rosa's unlisted number from a source at the telephone company, and on his way from the airport, he dialed it. Seven rings and then, "At the beep, speak." That's all. At the beep, Norman breathed suggestively into the phone and then whispered, "Rosa, buddy." A little forewarning that open war existed between them.

In the unzoned street behind and parallel with Rosa's there was an ancient car wash that looked like a covered bridge. Norman pulled into it, and phoned Rosa again.

"Hello."

"Did you get my message?"

"I found it derivative."

"Thank you."

"That was not a compliment."

"I know you have the old man."

"What do you intend to do about it?"

"I am already doing it. The house is surrounded. There are two ways of doing this. We can shoot our way in, creating a terrible mess, perhaps causing injury to innocent parties. Or you can come out with your hands over your head."

"There is a third possibility," Rosa said.

"What's that?"

"You and I can have a private talk about a lottery ticket."

"You have it?"

"The old man had it."

"Where?"

"In the pocket of his corduroy jacket."

"Which one?"

"The breast pocket, sometimes called the hankie pocket. Would you like me to read the very valuable numbers printed on that card?"

"What are you proposing?"

"We split."

"Together?"

"I meant we go fifty-fifty."

"What about Grandpa?"

"He's been as good as dead for weeks."

"You mean, do him like you did Edna?"

"Unless you can think of a better way."

"I don't know how I can explain this to the men deployed around your house."

"Cut the shit," she said. "You're sitting in your car alone, probably in the neighborhood."

"I'll be there in ten minutes."

"I'll be here."

What was she up to? It was possible that, whatever her original motive had been in taking Grandpa home, the lottery ticket had become her overriding goal. So why split with him? Because she knew what he knew about what she had done. Since the split was done under duress, she would try not to keep the deal. No doubt she already saw Norman Earwick doing a swan dive from the John Glenn Bridge into the Prune River. In sheer self-protection he would have to take out Rosa. If he was going to do any splitting, it would be with his client. She could cash the ticket without a hassle and they could all be rich as Rockefeller. Meanwhile there was Rosa Subiaco between him and that ticket. And of course Grandpa.

Norman eased his car out of the car wash and turned into the alley that ran behind Rosa's house. After fifty feet, he braked, the garage between him and the house. He did not notice the open garage on the other side of the alley in which a four-wheeled vehicle was parked deep and out of sight.

His cellular phone rang and he answered it if only to shut it up. Rosa spoke.

"You can leave your car right there."

"Where?"

"Behind the garage."

"How can you see it?"

"I saw you go out of sight and you haven't reappeared."

"Uh huh." Something in the side mirror caught his attention, but when he looked there was nothing. He turned off the motor. And then he saw Rosa standing beside his car, aiming a very ugly weapon at him.

"Get out of the car."

He reached for the key, but she had pulled open the door and jerked him out into the alley. The little gorilla was unbelievably strong. She had his arm twisted up behind his back as she pushed him into the darkness of the open garage. Norman was preparing a little speech that would get these negotiations onto a more favorable level when something crashed into his skull and the lights went out.

7

Nick's feature story on Rosa Subiaco was accepted by the major Fort Elbow paper but his triumph was somewhat dimmed when Norman Earwick's body was found floating in the Prune and caused the appearance of his story to be rescheduled. But there is always a silver lining. Nick saw the possibility of another great story, one that would rely on his personal acquaintance with the deceased. Lucy was numb with this addition to the litany of strange events.

"Nick, what is going on?"

Captain Manfredi and Homicide, not Missing Persons, took this case, since there was evidence that Norman had been hit on the head before being consigned to the deep. Nick was developing the habit of trying out possible phrases for future writing in actual speech.

"That refers to the ocean," Lucy told him.

"I'll work a variation on it." Nick spoke with the easy authority of the soon to be published writer. Rosa took the news well, almost too well.

"It will keep."

"I suppose I shouldn't resent the postponement," Nick said to his fellow author. "After all, I knew Earwick." When Rosa did not reply, he added "More or less."

The great attraction of a visit to Rosa was seeing her workroom again. It was like entering a chamber where every sound was absorbed and this took the resonance out of voices so that it was very much like telephone answering machines conversing. Rosa seemed buried away here, out of the reach of the world, so he told her all about Norman Earwick's demise.

He had parked his car on the bridge, something absolutely forbidden even in cases of emergency.

"Sort of a signal, I suppose. So that what he had done would be immediately clear."

"Any note?"

"Only a crazy message at his office. He had it rigged so he could record conversations with clients."

"With their knowledge?"

"Well, Lucy didn't know."

"What was the message?"

"He must have been losing it. He affected a female voice, but his secretary vouched for it being his. Apparently he had been playing games with her."

"Games?"

"On this apparatus. He staged an apparent break-in and then in this same voice whispered 'Rosebud.' Pretty corny."

"What does it mean?"

"Did you ever see Orson Wells in *Citizen Kane*?"

"Oh, of course. I see. But the message?"

"He said that for a long time he had been confused and troubled about his sexual orientation. Then he had a fit of giggling. But then he said it wasn't at all funny and could not live with himself any longer. He asked his clients to forgive him. It ended with the same sort of uncontrolled giggling."

"He sounds more drunk than confused."

"What is weird is that he apparently couldn't have committed suicide, unless he whacked his head on something while he fell."

"I suppose a fall like that does things to a body."

"They found him quickly because of his car."

"Well, you certainly have all the details."

He decided not to tell her of his plan to write a feature story about Norman Earwick. Nick was of course aware that she had given him extraordinary access, talked to him at length, shown interest in his work beyond the feature article devoted to her. He would have thought it was authorial vanity, but she seemed genuinely indifferent to the postponement of the story.

"As far as I can see, mine will be the first thing about you that isn't just about your books. Have you ever granted an interview before?"

"You are the first, Nick."

"Readers have insatiable appetites to know more about the writer of books they enjoy."

"That is not the insatiable appetite I address."

Nick managed a little laugh. He had fought his way through several of her novels and had to admit that for someone who lived such a solitary life she could sure write steamy scenes. Her critics claimed that she provided soft porn for the suburbs and her plots did have a way of being punctuated by scenes in which seduction or consummation or near rape were described in great detail. Nick had noticed in a library copy of her latest book a series of numbers. These turned out to refer to the pages where the sexy scenes began.

"You sure seem to know all about it."

"I did have a life before writing, Nick."

"Fred said you worked in the same realty office he does."

"In Toledo. Yes. He came to the talk I gave at the library."

"And bragged that you had signed a book for him."

"Did he say anything else?"

Nick looked puzzled.

185

"A woman cannot always rely on the man's discretion in these matters."

The lighting in the workroom was all artificial, since there were no windows, and the only lamps lit were those that illumined her desk and computer. Rosa herself sat in her work chair, a marvelously complicated piece of furniture that enabled her to maneuver quickly about the room and which rotated on command of buttons in the arms. Rosa and Nick sat at forty-five degree angles to one another as they had so often in the past and in this lighting Rosa looked as she had at the library the night she spoke. Then a hat had provided a mysterious setting for her face, now the lighting had the same effect.

"Have you talked to others about our sessions, Nick?"

"I have regarded them as confidential, except for what went into the feature, of course."

"You must have told Lucy."

"Maybe too much. She's pretty fed up with hearing about what I'm doing."

"Well, I suppose you've gotten ahead of her as a writer."

"Well . . ." Let it go. Rosa had said it. The change had not been so much in Lucy as in himself. He stopped talking about his project because she assumed he was coming to her for advice and this rankled. I mean, anything she said was borrowed from Mrs. McManus, and Mrs. McManus hadn't published anything for twenty-five years when she had been a regular book reviewer for the *Tribune*. Big deal. But she held forth about writing as if she had just descended from the mountain.

"Did I ever tell you about Mrs. McManus?"

"Do you show your work to her too?"

"I get her second hand from Lucy."

"Ah."

"Do you know of that woman in Terre Haute, Indiana,

who undertook to teach James Jones and a bunch of other guys writing? She had never written a word herself, there was no reason to think she knew any more about writing than the next person, but she put those guys through their paces, making them copy—literally copy—whole works of Hemingway so as to get the hang of his style."

"Holly something. She was interested in more than literature."

"Yeah."

"You mentioned they were all men. Her method was a species of domination, but she wanted to be dominated. She and Jones had an affair."

"I didn't know that."

"Where a man and a woman are concerned sex is always somewhere in the wings, Nick. And when creative work is involved, well, that is a powerful aphrodisiac."

"Afro . . . ?"

"Love potion."

Her chair was closer to his now. In the soundless room time seemed to have stopped. The boundaries of the room were the boundaries of the universe. Her fat little hand on his was soft and caressing. Nick's heart began to thump. Was she coming on to him? His only experience with sex had been in a western brothel when he was bumming back from a visit to California. He and Lucy were ardent but patient lovers. They would have it all in good time. That suddenly seemed selfish to Nick. A man wants a woman, a woman wants a man. It's as simple as that. Rosa was kneeling before his chair with her hands on his knees. She levered her face toward his and seemed to swallow him with her kiss. And then they were on the floor, rivaling one of Rosa's fictional scenes.

8

Fred went to the morgue with Alex to learn that the police had taken everything found in Earwick's pockets. They exchanged a look and headed for police headquarters. The first thing Fred had thought of when the news of Earwick came was the lottery ticket, and the same had been true of Alex, whom he had the good sense to call. Earwick's death, certainly no suicide, suggested that he had fallen afoul of those who had possession of the winning Power Ball ticket. He had called Lucy and told her he was closing in on those who had Grandpa. Well, they had apparently closed in on him first. Given that he had been found in the river, it was highly unlikely that he would have gained possession of the ticket, but there might be some indication of whom he had suspected of having it and Grandpa.

Manfredi of Homicide was a man from whom thirty plus years as a policeman had wrung any capacity for surprise, dismay or disgust at what human beings are capable of doing to one another. He had thick hair that was making an easy transition from black to gray, his moustache was theatrical and his bulging eyes looked out over half-glasses perched near the tip of his meaty nose. He smoked with the pleasure of one who knew that most things were dangerous to his health. He had in his desk a list of murder victims who had quit smoking in order to prolong their lives.

"What's your connection with the deceased?"

"We were clients of his."

"We."

"My niece had hired him on family business."

"Is she here?"

"You have to realize that this death is only the most recent in a series of things that have upset her greatly."

Alex said, "And I represent the family."

"So what do you want?"

Fred let Alex do the talking, assuming he had a better chance of piercing the complete indifference with which Manfredi regarded them. Alex began with Grandpa and Manfredi had smoked three cigarettes and was lighting a fourth by the time Alex brought it to the discovery of the body of Norman Earwick.

"He had a severe injury to his head," Manfredi said. "Who would want to get rid of him?" He looked from Fred to Alex as if sizing them up for the role.

"He had called Lucy Yates earlier on the day he apparently met his death to tell her that he was certain he had located her grandfather and was about to rescue him."

"That all?"

"That's all."

"Wasn't Missing Persons looking into that?" His sardonic smile seemed to invite their criticisms of this department, but Alex did not take the bait.

"With what has happened, the family is more than ever concerned about the grandfather."

"That was how long ago, two weeks? He's probably dead."

"No body has shown up."

"That happens. Sometimes a farmer plowing a field will turn up a corpse missing for decades."

"That's a cheerful thought."

"I'm not trying to cheer you up. I'm telling you what experience tells me."

"What was found on the body of Earwick?"

Manfredi picked up a phone and a cigarette and a half hour later a uniformed cop dropped a plastic evidence bag on his desk. Manfredi spilled the contents before him, and held up a hand, indicating that nothing was to be touched. He himself was pulling on what he called his digital condoms, white latex gloves.

There was a wallet containing credit cards, thirty-three dollars, some business cards of Earwick's own and a receipt for a rental car. Manfredi unfolded it and cocked back his head, the better to utilize his half glasses.

"The same day. Funny."

"He rented a car the day he was killed."

"That's what it says." He jiggled the receipt.

"But his own car was parked on the bridge."

"Yup."

"What's it mean?"

"We'll find out." Manfredi pushed back from his desk, rose and patted his shirt pocket to make sure his cigarettes were there, and looked at Fred and Alex, "You can check with me later."

Alex was leaning over the desk, studying the other things that had been in the evidence bag. Manfredi scooped them up and sealed the bag and took it with him as they left his office.

"What do you think?" Fred asked Alex.

"It's in their hands now."

"What else was in that bag?"

"Some Rolaids and a phone number."

"I wonder whose it was?"

Alex pulled out the little notebook in which he had written

when they parted from Manfredi and showed Fred the telephone number. "We can find out."

But when they tried the number they found that it had been discontinued nor would the company tell them whose number it had been.

Fred could not help wondering if Alex was too interested in that lottery money. The visit to Manfredi, particularly watching the items found on the body of Norman Earwick unceremoniously dumped on the desk, gave Fred a powerful sense of the dangers of pursuing unearned and undeserved money. After all, it had very likely been that Power Ball ticket far more than finding Grandpa that had motivated Earwick and brought him to a watery grave. Fred was glad when the telephone number wrote *finis* to their efforts.

"I don't know about you, Alex, but I have to get back to earning an honest living."

"I thought you sold houses."

"Ho ho."

And so they parted and Fred drove off to see Hazel. The uxorious impulse was strong in him. That is what had kept him married to Edna through thick and thin and that is what explained the almost domestic arrangement he had fallen into with Hazel. Hazel was good to him in a way that Edna had not been, but then Hazel was not his wife. Who knew what transformations a marriage license would effect in her. Fred could still remember the surprise he had felt when the warm and cuddly girl he had married turned into the harridan who was his wife. He had no assurance that there was not a similar Delilah lurking behind Hazel's easy going sensuality. Fred had always felt that he had the better of their arrangement and perhaps Hazel had thought so too. In any case, Fred intended to move with circumspection. Pleasant as the

191

prospect of formalizing his relation with Hazel was, moving in with her and both of them moving to Toledo, he would not have the excuse of age and inexperience if he made a second mistake. And Hazel had already made two of her own.

Realizing that he could easily face a future that did not involve the impossible riches of that Power Ball ticket made him feel almost virtuous. Of course he could not really believe that such a sum was within reach of Lucy and that some portion of it would surely trickle down to him. That kind of money spelled trouble. How many lottery winners ended up happier than they were before? Besides, the death of Edna would bring him her insurance money, no small sum, though minuscule by Power Ball standards. He had his job, he had his health, and he had Hazel. Let Alex worry about where that winning ticket had ended up.

He turned on his beeper as he drove and almost immediately it went off. He picked up the phone and called the office.

"Fred. You got a message for me?"

"Just a minute, sweetie," Dolores said, as sweet as her three hundred pounds would suggest. "Here it is. Nick says call. You want his number?"

"Let me have it."

"You'll have to be more specific."

Ye gods. The thought of wallowing in the mountain of flesh Dolores was alarmed him. On the other hand . . . But she was reading off the numbers.

It was an anxious Nick who answered his phone on the first ring. "I've got to talk to you."

"Well, at the moment I am on my way to Toledo."

"Where can I meet you?"

Visions of dalliance with Hazel were threatened but Fred could not ignore the urgency in Nick's voice.

"Well, there is a mall in West Toledo where we could have a cup of coffee."

"I know it well. Name the coffee shop and I'll be there before you are."

"Where are you?"

Nick named the mile sign he had last passed, and that put him maybe twenty miles behind. The name of Hazel's fast-food place was almost on his tongue, but Fred decided against it.

"The Star Trek Café."

"I'll be there."

Fred's guess that it was some kind of trouble with Lucy was not far wrong. An anguished Nick laid his hands flat on the table between them. "I'm not worthy of her, Fred. I've betrayed her."

"What have you done?"

"I did it with another woman."

Was he saying that he had also done it with Lucy? Fred did not want to know. Feeling like one who is not without sin himself he said, "Tell me all about it."

Fred hoped God finds our transgressions as innocent as he found Nick's. Nick was taking all the blame but it sounded to Fred as if the woman, older than Nick, had seduced the boy. Hearing confessions must be like this.

"Don't see her again, Nick. That's the solution."

"No, that's the problem."

Nick had begun by saying that he would never divulge the woman's name, and he stuck with it when Fred said give me a clue.

"You mean you're going to go see her and go through this again? Let me tell you something, Nick. You feel bad now, but you'll get used it. In time it won't seem so bad to you.

Finally it won't seem bad at all. That's the road you're starting down."

"I wish it was that simple."

"It is. Now."

After they parted, Fred sauntered through the mall, on his way to let Hazel know he was in town.

"She didn't come in today."

He called her apartment but there was no answer. He tried again several times from different phones in the mall and then on his own phone when he went out to his car. And then he saw her. She was with someone but then he was gone. A young man. She pushed through the doors and came toward him, good old Hazel, warm, receptive, smiling. Fred was more reflective. For a moment he had thought that was Nick she was talking to inside.

"They said you didn't come in today."

"That's what I told them to say. But they weren't supposed to say it to you."

"Trying to avoid someone?"

"Avoidance is the farthest thing from my mind," she cooed, snuggling closer as he drove away.

Fred was thinking of things he might have told Nick.

9

Afterward, Nick had actually cried and then began to apologize to her for taking advantage of her that way. Rosa was certain this was some kind of joke but he persisted in contrition and she found she liked the role he had cast her in.

"You're so impetuous."

"It's different for a man."

It was odd to be instructed in the difference between the sexes by such a calf. There was every indication that this had been his first sexual experience and he wanted to tell her what it was like.

"I guess a woman wants to be taken," she said.

But he was almost shocked by this. My God, he knew the kind of fiction she wrote, did he expect her to talk like a bride? It had been fun, but she did not propose to spend the rest of the day listening to him bewail the fact that he had violated her hospitality. What an ass. This was a new experience for Rosa. In the past, making love had always been the prelude to disgust on her partner's behalf. Julius had been different of course, but Julius was blind. As passion cooled her hitherto ardent lovers had been unable to disguise their true reaction to her looks. That had sealed their fate of course. Earwick, the private investigator, had been a special case.

She had expected a more challenging encounter but it had been child's play to pull him from the car and hustle him into the darkened garage where her four-wheeler was parked. She hit him over the head with the gun and brought him down. This was easier than she would have expected. She looked at his car visible through the open door as if it were on display. Dragging him out to the car was more work than he was worth. The keys were still in the ignition. She drove the car ahead a few yards and put it into reverse. As she was backing it into the garage opening Earwick came staggering into view. She gunned the motor and pinned him in before he could get away. All the fight had gone out of him. She opened the trunk and told him to get in. His main worry seemed to be that she would hit him on the head again. She did, when she parked on the bridge and went around and unlocked the trunk. She could still feel the strain of dragging him to the railing and tipping him over for the long fall into the dark waters below.

She left the car and then caught a bus, and transferred downtown. It was a short walk from the bus stop to her house. And there was Grandpa, sitting where she had left him, staring uncomprehendingly at the television. What difference did it make whether it was on or off. He had wet his pants, however, but she had been gone a long time. She got him into his pajamas and put him to bed, then poured a bourbon and 7-Up and settled down to think.

The lottery ticket had been in Grandpa's pocket, as Lucy had said, and it was indeed the winner of several weeks ago. Fifty-six million dollars. It was that rather than his having been hired to find the old man that explained Earwick's willingness to face her on her own turf, particularly when he knew what he evidently did know. The ticket, she decided, was worthless to her. Of course it was difficult to look at it and realize that it was worth such an amount. Rosa did not need money. She made lots and spent hardly anything, since she just went from book to book and never took time to enjoy herself.

The problem of course was herself. Imagine someone like her on a cruise ship or at a resort. She would be a figure of fun and what kind of relaxation was that. No, the lottery ticket would have to be returned with Grandpa.

Rosa felt an understandable satisfaction in having achieved what she had set out to do. From the moment she realized that the old man was being deliberately abandoned there in the parking lot in West Toledo, Rosa had vowed to rescue the man and make the woman who had abandoned him pay. She had done both. So why not just put Grandpa in the four-wheeler with the lottery ticket in his pocket and deliver him to his granddaughter?

She had to restore things to *status quo ante*—minus a few people—in such a way that no one would ever connect her with Grandpa. One of the benefits of turning Nick into a confidant, aside from being kept informed of things on the other side, was that, if it came to that, Nick's visits to her house would argue powerfully for her innocence. How could a young man visit her so often and be unaware of an old man in the house, an old man he himself knew?

But Rosa did not want it to come to that. What she needed was something comparable to the successful and satisfying resolution of one of her more complicated plots. And to come up with that, she needed a good night's sleep.

She dreamed, tenderly, of Nick and rather than put the dream away in order to put her mind to the task of tying up loose ends, she permitted the dream to suggest the course she might take. Having Nick on the floor of her study in the rough and tumble of passion had seemed a one-time thing, the satisfaction of curiosity as well as desire. She had wanted to know what a man that age would be like. Her previous companions had all been a trifle long in tooth, and if the impatient ardor of his youth had made their lovemaking a small thing when measured by the clock, it had made up in passion for its brevity. Rosa realized that she had for the first time met in the flesh a man of the median age of her heroes. Were her stories truly worthy of what such a man could do?

This question did not lead on to the creative impulse, writing out the answer as her fingers flew across the keyboard of her computer. She found that she wanted Nick again. She began to think of keeping him, not in the way she had kept Julius or Grandpa, but holding him by catering to the impetuous needs of his flesh.

It was an occupational hazard that Rosa now thought in the charged phrases in which she wrote. She was, as she might have written, filled with foreboding but also with excitement when she turned her eyes, brimming with tears of hope, glistening with love, to the perilous future.

Part Five

CATCH

.

1

"I want to go to law school," Lucy said, sitting across the desk from Alex. She had shaken her head vigorously when he suggested that they repair to the matching chairs in the corner of his office, a sign that this was a serious call. Her mouth was set, her eyes directly on him.

"I thought you wanted to be a writer."

"So did I. That all seems so childish now. I want to live in the real world, the way you do."

"Law comes into play when the real world breaks down, Lucy. It is people with ordinary jobs, living in ordinary houses, raising a family, who are in the real world."

"No one has proposed to me."

"But I thought you and Nick . . ."

"Alex, he is childish. For weeks the center of his life has been a feature story on the author of romance novels, novels he probably couldn't stand reading, and yet he celebrates her as if she were Edith Wharton."

"All the changes that have taken place needn't change you, Lucy."

"I think they have just helped me get rid of a veneer."

"What does Nick think of this?"

"I have no idea."

"You haven't discussed it with him?"

"Discussed? With Nick? With Nick you listen about all the

wonderful things he is doing, and it is against the rules to comment in a way that might be thought critical."

"You've had a fight."

"I wish we had. Oh, Alex, where is Grandpa?"

She began to sob helplessly and he came around the desk and tentatively put his hand on her shoulder. She slumped against him and his hand traveled across her back to the other shoulder. He stopped breathing, but she continued to sob. He bent and pressed his forehead to her hair.

"You poor thing, you poor thing."

His words had the effect of reminding her of all the sadness in her life. When the sobbing subsided, she sat back and looked at him through the tears.

"Tell me about my father."

He took her hand and led her to the corner of the office where they could both sit and told her about her father. But it was his own story too, his life had been interwoven with Don's and then they had met her mother.

"I loved her, Lucy, but she loved your father."

And why shouldn't she? Don had not flinched when the chance came to serve his country and Vivian had watched him go off, holding Lucy in her arms, not knowing that this was their final farewell, and so soon.

"I was too cowardly to do what he did. Maybe I was proving that your mother was right to prefer him."

"You were always so close, one of the family, yet . . ."

"Yet not. I dedicated myself to your mother and to you. But I did not dare to get too close."

"You still loved her."

"I always loved her. People want to think that we get a second chance in life, but I don't think we ever do."

"You wanted to marry her."

"I never told her."

His confession of failure and foolishness had an unexpected effect. She took his hand and held it in both of hers and looked at him as if he were a hero rather than a coward. And then impulsively she kissed him.

"Poor Alex."

"Poor Lucy."

They looked at one another and then stood and she came easily into his arms and he held her, not knowing whether he was still just Uncle Alex or something more. When she stepped back, he said, "You'll have to take the LSAT if you're going to apply for law school."

She waved it away with a laugh. "You're right. I'm just going through a phase."

After she left, Alex pulled on a hinged shelf in the bookcase behind his desk and a row of books swung out revealing several bottles of vintage liquor. Alex selected the Amontillado and poured himself two ounces of this precious liquid. He put the shelf back in place and took his glass to where he had sat with Lucy, where she had looked at him with an expression that might have been love. He lifted the glass and then drank to his fears. Beware of answered prayers.

The following day, Fred called to say he wanted to break the seal of the confessional and told him the story that a very distraught Nick had told him.

"Wild oats," Alex opined.

"That was my first reaction too."

"What was your second?"

"I asked myself if this was the guy I wanted marrying Lucy. What do you think?"

"I think that's up to her."

"But he isn't likely to tell her about this."

"I hope not."

"Of course a lot depends on who the other woman is."

"How so?"

"Alex, the way he tells it, she came on to him. He might think of it as a solitary fall, but will she? And when I asked him if he would see her again he made it pretty clear that he would."

"Of course, if it becomes another woman and not just a lapse."

Alex did not like the thoughts that were stirred up in him by this revelation. Lucy had come to him yesterday with a grievance against Nick. Could it be that what she mentioned and what was really bothering her were not the same thing? Did she already know of this woman?

But he also felt that he was the male counterpart of this older woman and his prey was Lucy. How would Fred react if he knew the frustrated hopes he had harbored all his life?

2

Fred had never been jealous of Edna, God knows, what occasion for it would there have been, and for Hazel he had been a bit of luck as she had been for him. Oh, they got along and it was steady but there was no understanding between them. Hadn't he considered and then rejected the thought of formalizing their relationship? Of course he had just assumed that, for all her voiced disinclination to marrying again, she would have jumped at the chance. He had always assumed that he was the only man in her life. And now there definitely was someone else.

He spied on her. He told her he had to spend the day in Fort Elbow and then he hung around the mall, careful to keep out of sight, and when she went home at night he sat in his car outside the familiar building and waited. And waited, but no one showed up. And then it happened. She swung out of her place of work with a young man on her arm, laughing into his face, wiggling her ass as they went off. The young man was Nick.

Fred tried to remember the abject penitent who had blurted out the dreadful sins he had committed with an older woman. He recalled word by bitter word the account of how the woman had seduced him. What the hell was going on? Was Fred supposed to guess that the woman was Hazel? He felt dizzy at the thought that Hazel and Nick had entered into a conspiracy to torture him. Did letting him in on it, however obliquely, add zest to their affair?

He felt like a fool, calling Alex with such a tale, but he relied on the lawyer's devotion to Lucy and remembrance of her mother. To no avail. If Lucy were to be told, it would to be by himself. And would this have the desired effect? What was the desired effect? He wanted Hazel for himself alone. He could not meet her now and go on as if he did not know of her perfidy.

He was distracted from these maddening thoughts by a message from Manfredi, the homicide detective who has investigating the death of Earwick.

"I mentioned that Earwick had rented a car."

"Yes."

"When I looked into it, I learned that your wife had rented a car on the night the old man disappeared. What was that all about?"

"I haven't the faintest idea. You must be mistaken. Edna had her own car."

"So did Earwick. Oh, there's no doubt your wife rented a car that night, even if she did do so in the name of your niece."

"Lucy!"

"It was her not returning the gas can that had enabled her to start her car. It was in the lot and out of gas. This was about 10 PM."

"The gas can!"

"You know about it."

"It's a crazy story."

"Tell it to me."

Fred had come to Manfredi's office and it seemed a less macabre, more efficient place on this occasion. He was impressed by all the bustle, people coming and going, phones ringing. He had formed his view of the police from their experience with Missing Persons. He relayed to Manfredi as accurately as he remembered the disappearing and reappearing gas can.

"Whatever happened to it?"

"I gave it to Earwick."

Manfredi looked at him for a moment and then picked up his phone to ask someone named Childs if there had been a red gas can in Earwick's office, car or apartment. He listened, not looking at Fred. He hung up.

"It seems to have disappeared again."

Manfredi suggested that they repair to O'Boyle's across the way and have a drink. "Not that there is a helluva lot to celebrate. You seem to know as much about what has been going on as anyone."

They settled in a booth, with glasses of Guinness before them on which foam as thick as marshmallow had formed. Manfredi drained a third of his glass and then set it down with the look of a man who would shortly pick it up again.

"It is Earwick's death I am investigating but it sits atop an extraordinary sequence of events involving your family. The grandfather disappears mysteriously from the house, an old man with Alzheimer's who has yet to be found. The report has it that your wife was alone with him at the house and that his disappearance was discovered the following morning. What the report neglects to say is that your wife left the house, drove to the airport, rented a car in her niece's name and sometime later returned it and when she claimed her own car found that it was out of gas. The pay booths have gas for such contingencies, she borrowed a can of gas, got her car started and when she paid promised to return the can filled with gas. The fact that she never did led to the strange things you have told me of."

"You are suggesting that my wife took Grandpa somewhere and let him out and then returned home, managing to
get there before Lucy and I returned from a lecture in
Toledo?"

"A lecture."

"A woman author who writes under the name of Rosa
Charrin was giving a talk in the library."

"And you drove all that way to hear her."

"I work in Toledo. This woman used to work in the same
place."

"And you just wanted to see her again?"

"She has been phenomenally successful."

"Spell her name for me." Manfredi wrote it down.

"Her real name is Rosa Subiaco."

"Why the alias?"

"It's a pen name."

"Why did your niece go all that way to hear her?"

"She went with a friend of hers. They think they want to
become writers."

"Male, female?"

"The friend? Nick Byers."

Manfredi wrote that down too. For the first time Fred had
the sense that someone seriously wanted to discover what had
been going on.

"Back to your wife. Do you think that she took the old man
out and abandoned him somewhere?"

Fred continued to drink from his glass. He swallowed and
put it down. "Yes. I have come to believe that. The business
with the gas can played on her sense of guilt and drove her out
of her mind."

"I don't think she committed suicide."

"You don't!"

"You gave testimony that she was heavily sedated. The

open door and leaving without taking anything with her, her purse, whatever, suggests she was taken into custody."

"By?"

"By whoever was teasing her with the gas can."

"Someone at the airport?"

Manfredi shook his head. "I doubt it. Apparently Earwick got lucky and figured out who was playing games with the gas can. And he got what your wife got."

"But who is it?"

"It's not you, is it?"

"Good God, no."

"Want another?" Flourishing his empty glass.

"No. What are you up to next?"

"I want to go over Earwick's office."

Fred left Manfredi with an altered estimate of the man. Had he been serious in asking if Fred had been the one driving Edna nuts with that gas can? But it was the detective's conviction that Edna had been killed that struck him. Who would want to kill Edna? People might say that if anyone had a reason to wish her dead, it was himself, and he had to admit that he had not mourned when she was gone. But he could never have physically harmed her. Of course it was idle to think he had done so, unless you imagined there had been a conspiracy between him and Nick and Lucy to create a story about being in Toledo to cover getting rid of Edna. Crazy. Apparently Edna had left a trail that night all too easy to discover. Manfredi had discovered it. And someone else had too, the one who had killed Edna and Norman Earwick.

3

When Rosa first thought of proposing a trade, Grandpa for Nick, it had seemed a joke, but since, it had settled into the serious backdrop of what she was planning to do.

She would restore Grandpa to Lucy. Lucy was just someone Nick talked about, in a smarmy way at first, but now with a more critical edge to his voice, an edge aided by wine, the muted lights of her workroom and the thick sponge mattress on the floor. Rosa had found the infallible path to a man's heart. He was hooked on her. And she was hooked on him. In the bathroom, after a shower, she would wipe the steam from the mirror and watch her unadorned self appear. Her hair curled when wet but this gave it the look of a wig, her face even in repose had a worried expression, her cheeks pushing up against her eyes, her nose bulbous, her mouth generous, a mouth that deserved a better face. The rest of her anatomy was a study in beach balls. She raised her short arms and watched her mammoth breasts rise. Her navel was hidden in a fold of fat. How had so much talent been imprisoned in such a body?

But with the right lighting, alcohol in the blood and the sure ally of his concupiscence, she had linked Nick to her with hoops of steel. She had not only changed her cellular number, she had subscribed with a different company. A precaution after Earwick found her unlisted number. Only Nick had her number. She told him this in a husky whisper.

"Amphibole is the fun of language."

"Geez, I wish I had your vocabulary."

"You will."

Pygmalion in reverse? Why not? She would mold him to her own specifications. No fiction, though, he hadn't the least idea about fiction. Not that they wasted much time on such subjects anymore.

"Doesn't Lucy wonder where you are?"

"She's studying." He rolled onto his back. "She's changed since her grandfather left."

"Left?"

"Whatever."

"What do you think happened to him?"

"Rosa, I'll tell you something. I really don't care anymore. How long can you make an absence the center of your life? Lucy can do that but I can't. I won't. He has to be dead, doesn't he? He couldn't take care of himself for a full day and he has been gone nearly a month."

"You may be right."

The little lights embedded in the ceiling of her workroom were arranged like the starry skies above. Nick had not noticed the Big Dipper, Ursa Major and Minor or the North Star until she pointed them out.

"That's something I'd like to learn. Astronomy."

Maybe he meant astrology, you never knew with Nick. This was someone who went to college? She had told him she was an autodidact and he reacted as if she had told him she had herpes. But his education could await the passing of their honeymoon. How else think of the exploratory wildness with which they whiled away hours on the sponge mattress.

Rosa became careless. Whenever Nick called, she said,

yes, of course, I'm here. Then he showed up without calling first, and she had been delightfully surprised rather than concerned. And then one afternoon, while a spent Rosa fell asleep, Nick went off to the bathroom and decided to explore the old house in which he was spending so much time but of which he had seen little more than Rosa's workroom.

He looked at her kitchen, equipped for a chef; he saw without appreciation her dining set, nor did the antiques in the living room and salon arrest his attention. Her plants in the sunroom, but how many could he have named? He was like a savage looking uncomprehendingly at civilization. He looked everywhere. And inevitably he opened the door of the room where Grandpa was.

Imagine the half-dressed young man staring into the vacant eyes of an old man who had been the object of such frantic concern for weeks. Disbelief gives way to the evidence of his eyes.

Does he rush to the old man, take him in his arms, carry him if necessary to his car and drive him off to his loved ones?

Does he shout in surprise and confront Rosa with his discovery?

Do a thousand pieces of the puzzle suddenly come together and he flees the house, more worried about himself than the old man?

None of the above.

She was wakened when he tumbled in beside her and pulled her arm over him, a child returned to its mother.

"I found Grandpa."

She said nothing.

"You've had him all along."

"I rescued him when Edna abandoned him."

"But why keep him?"

"I decided to keep him until I had punished Edna."

He lay still. Finally, he was beginning to see the pattern in the events of the past month. Now he knew he was lying in the arms of a woman who had passed sentence on Edna and then executed that sentence. She could almost hear his thoughts. What would be his reaction now?

He snuggled more closely against her.

"Rosa, what are we going to do?"

But the problem was hers, not theirs. His discovery of Grandpa changed everything. Rosa stared at the simulated night sky above her and tried to read the portents. But it had nothing to do with the stars. She had blundered out of hubris. She had trusted too much to Nick's lack of curiosity, general dimness and her own ability to keep awake while he was in the house. Now he knew everything, or at least he had the premise from which everything else followed. He had already confessed that he was sick and tired of worrying about the old man, but that had been on the assumption that the old man was dead. It was silly to think that her secret was safe with him or with anyone else.

"I think we need a little drink," she said, getting up and padding off to the kitchen.

She poured two glasses of wine. On the way back to the workroom, she stopped at the bathroom and took a bottle from the cabinet and poured half its contents into one of the glasses. When Nick took the glass, she raised hers.

"To us."

He was soon unconscious. With a sigh, Rosa picked him up and carried him to the quarters in the basement, which had once housed Julius Sweeney. Of course Julius had been blind and that sufficed to keep him in place. Poor Nick, wearing only skivvies, had to be made secure. When she snapped a handcuff on his wrist and snapped the other around the pipe on which Julius had beaten so plaintively she hoped she could find the key to the cuffs.

She dressed and with the keys she had taken from Nick's trousers went out to his car. This turn of events had rendered obsolete the plan she had been formulating and now she was improvising, always dangerous. She started the car and drove to the John Glenn Bridge over the Prune River where she abandoned Nick's car not far from where Earwick's was found.

It was a long walk to a bus stop and a long wait for the bus but thanks to public transportation she got safely home.

Later, when she was at work at her computer, a clanking sound began to rise from the basement.

4

Manfredi assumed an air of calm imperturbability while everyone around him was spinning out of control. The discovery of Nick's abandoned car on the bridge over the Prune had set off an unsuccessful search for the body and a chorus of indignant protest from concerned citizens, chief among them the remaining members of the family which somehow seemed at the center of these weird events and their legal representative. He was currently explaining to Alex Schuler what was being done.

"The car is with the lab now. Something will turn up, count on it." The confidence in his voice was not what he felt.

"Lucy is under sedation. How much can that young woman be expected to endure?"

"Weren't they engaged?"

"No!"

"I only asked." Alex seemed almost insulted by the question. "I thought I had been told that."

"Nick has been seeing another woman. An older woman."

"How do you know that?"

"I tell you because it seems relevant now. And also because it explains why I reacted to your question as I did."

"How did you find out about this other woman?"

"Fred told me. In confidence. But the circumstances absolve me of keeping it secret."

"How did Fred find out?"

"He told me," Fred said. "He came to me and broke down and told me he had made love to an older woman. He was abject. He thought it was a solitary fall."

"Wasn't it?"

"I think it became a habit."

"Did he tell you who the woman was?"

"I think I know."

Manfredi waited while Fred went *mano a mano* with himself in a moral debate he could not lose. And then he gave Manfredi the name.

Hazel Yzerman managed a fast food restaurant in the shopping mall in West Toledo and seemed delighted that Manfredi had come by to see her. She had her hair pulled back and plaited in a single braid and this gave her a youthful look. And she was expressive. Whenever she spoke, her hand went out to touch his arm.

"What brings you over here?"

"This is the mall where an old man was abandoned."

"There are a lot of abandoned old men in this place." Hand on arm.

Manfredi asked her if she knew a young man named Nick Byers.

"The college kid?"

"How do you happen to know him?"

"He edits the mall newsletter. He's also writing some newspaper story, or says he is. He wanted to talk, so we talked." Nothing in her manner suggested that there was anything more than that.

"I am looking into several recent deaths, bodies found in the river. Have you heard of those?"

She became wary. "What about them?"

216

"I believe you know the husband of the woman who was killed."

"I thought she committed suicide."

"That was a preliminary verdict."

"My God."

"That clears the way for you and Fred."

She slapped him. Her hand coming at him so fast from the other side of the booth he couldn't have avoided it even if it hadn't surprised the hell out of him.

"I'm not accusing you of anything." His cheek stung but he would be damned if he would give her the satisfaction of showing it.

"Just Fred?"

He liked her. It seemed a shame that Fred didn't trust her. The tip about Nick's hot affair with an older woman clearly had nothing to do with Hazel. That is what he had come to find out. But he wouldn't want to be around the next time Fred and Hazel got together.

However false that Hazel had been initiating Nick into the deeper mysteries of the flesh, Fred thought so and that gave Manfredi pause. But Nick was still just missing, his body had not been discovered and while it seemed only a matter of time until it was found and examined, Manfredi was going to leave things as they were. Meanwhile he could puzzle over what he had learned listening to the tapings made of conversations in Earwick's office.

Mrs. Barnacle was more than helpful although, as she said, she wasn't sure she even worked there any more.

"I've already applied for unemployment."

"What was he like?"

"I never worked for anyone like him before. He seemed to have this picture of himself that he carried around like an invisible mirror and he was always checking himself out in it, wondering how he was doing."

"No confidence?"

"Oh he had confidence enough for three. It was vanity."

"Did he have a lot of business?"

"Not since I've been here."

"Help me get this thing working, will you."

And soon the office was filled with the voice of the late Norman Earwick. She shuddered. "He's talking to himself. He did that a lot. I think the main reason he had this system put in was so he could listen to himself."

But the taping was recent and Earwick was talking about the work he was doing for Lucy Yates.

"Rosebud is the clue," Earwick said, *"It's nuts to think it refers to a movie."*

"That's what I told him," Mrs. Barnacle whispered as if she thought her late boss might hear her.

"Citizen Kane."

"He didn't know that."

"Why is it a clue?"

"When the office was broken into, that word was recorded. I'll show you."

She changed cassettes, fast forwarded a bit, and then the room was filled with the sound of breathing. Just when Manfredi thought she had made a mistake the room was filled with the whispered word. Rosebud.

"Play it again."

She did. He had her turn it off. "Tell me about the break-in."

"The only thing missing was the clothes."

"The clothes."

"Mister Earwick had asked Lucy to bring some clothes of her grandfather's. That was just to let them know he was hard at work. They were in the closet, on the shelf."

"Some missing clothes and Rosebud?"

She nodded. "My next job I want something absolutely routine. I thought this would be romantic, full of adventure."

"How many secretaries have a boss get killed?"

She nodded with raised brows, as if she had to concede that.

"Do you have files on the Grandpa case?"

She rolled backward and pulled open a file cabinet. She hummed as she flipped through the folders, then stopped humming. She was backtracking. She looked at him, the corners of her mouth pulled down. "They're gone."

She couldn't remember if she had checked the files after the break-in but was sure that was when they had to have been removed.

"Maybe Earwick took them."

She laughed and began tapping her forehead. "He said his records were up here. The files are no great loss though. They were just transcriptions I did of the tapes. I mean, I had to do something or I'd go nuts."

They went back to the tape where Earwick was summing up what he knew, the summary that began with the remark that Rosebud was the clue. Mrs. Barnacle said she hadn't typed that one up yet.

Earwick spoke at great length of the Grandpa case, as he called it, leaving nothing implicit, though he starred in all stages of the narrative. Mrs Barnacle lifted her eyes and said she was going to lunch.

"Do you want anything?"

"I'm on a diet."

"Who isn't?"

"Bring me a hamburger."

It was painful listening at such length to Earwick's fruity account of where he was at this point. He repeated a cellular number several times, but this was the discontinued number. The holder of that number according to Earwick was Rosa Subiaco.

Manfredi turned off the tape.

He was sitting in Earwick's chair staring vacantly before him when Mrs Barnacle came back.

"Did you hear?"

"What?"

"The old man is back. He just showed up at his house."

5

Lucy had been reduced to a condition not unlike that of Aunt Edna in her last days. How could anyone take so much? From the time Grandpa had disappeared her life had been spiraling from one bad thing to another. It had been dreadful to see Edna give way under the strain as she had, but now Lucy was told that her death had not been suicide. Someone had dragged her out of the house and carried her away to throw her into the river. Lucy cried out involuntarily when she thought of her poor aunt dying so cruel and horrible a death. She had not been an amiable person, perhaps, but no one deserved to die so violently. Then it was Earwick, the man she had counted on to find Grandpa, killed in a manner that recalled Edna's death. People spoke of a pattern in these events but no one could tell her what on earth they meant. The news that Nick was missing was the last straw.

She actually collapsed. She had never fainted in her life before but she was not ashamed that the news about Nick had floored her. Alex, who had brought the news, carried her to her bed and when she came to, he sat beside her, pressing a cold cloth to her forehead.

"I can't take any more."

His hand left the cloth and traveled into her hair, combing it back with his fingers. Lucy closed her eyes. Had her father soothed her like this when she was a child?

"Try not to think of it."

"What else can I think of? Have they found him yet?"

"No. The currents are tricky there."

She shuddered and turned toward him and he pressed his forehead to her hair. Alex was all she had left, it seemed, the one link to her mother and father and to Grandpa. The thought of the poor helpless old man brought on tears. Her eyes were full of tears when she turned and imagined she saw Grandpa standing in the doorway.

She closed her eyes. She mustn't go mad as Edna did. She would not have hallucinations. Slowly she opened her eyes again. He was still there.

"Grandpa!"

He remembered her, she knew he did. She scrambled across the bed and threw her arms around him and it didn't frighten him a bit. Alex said, "My God in heaven. It is him."

The next ten minutes marked a time of high elation. From the depths Lucy had been raised abruptly to the heights. What she had hoped and prayed for during all these awful weeks had been granted. Grandpa was home! She kissed him, she made him a bowl of the cereal with raisons he liked, she sat him at the kitchen table and fussed over him. All the while, Alex was there in the background, allowing her to let herself go with joy. Next she took Grandpa to his room and made him look around. And then, a miracle, he looked at Lucy and smiled.

And then of course Alex asked the obvious question.

"How the hell did he get here?"

While Lucy had fussed over Grandpa, he had checked out front and out back, but there was no unexplained vehicle.

"You'd think he'd been next door all this while."

He repeated that after Captain Manfredi arrived, thus generating useless errands for the colleagues who soon joined Manfredi. The neighbors were as nonplused as anyone, and while scarcely as ecstatic as Lucy were glad that the old man was back.

Just like that. Manfredi shook his head, and Alex asked him when anything else about the disappearance had made sense.

"You have a point."

Fred made it back from Toledo in record time. He gave Manfredi a dirty look but then he just stood staring at Grandpa, grinning like the Cheshire cat.

"Did you check?" he asked Lucy.

"Check?"

Fred leaned forward and slipped two long fingers into the breast pocket of Grandpa's corduroy jacket. When he withdrew them they held a lottery ticket.

"Voilá."

They all looked at the colorful piece of pasteboard that was worth fifty-six million dollars. Even Grandpa looked at. And smiled once more at Lucy.

"He remembers," she cried. She took him in her arms once more. "That's our ticket, remember. Share and share alike."

"Why don't you give that to Alex for safekeeping," Fred suggested.

But Alex read the back of the ticket and went off to make a phone call to the state lottery commission.

There seemed to be no way to keep the media out of this and Lucy did not begrudge it. For once they had something to celebrate. The only annoyance was that they showed more interest in the lottery ticket than they did in Grandpa's being home again.

"I suppose you'll make a considerable donation to Alzheimer's research," one bright thing said.

It was the first in what would be hundreds of unbidden

223

suggestions Lucy would receive on how to use the money. She didn't want to think about the money. Let Alex and Fred take care of it.

Finally she got away with Grandpa and they sat in his room.

"Where have you been?" she asked.

He responded, but it was with a request that he be taken to the bathroom.

Alone, she thought. Only hours ago Alex was telling me to think about something other than Nick. Grandpa's return was about the only thing that could have enabled her to do that. Less frantically now she could worry about Nick. After Grandpa's return, she refused to believe that he was dead. He was alive, somewhere, and like Grandpa he would come back to her.

6

Rosa missed the old man almost as soon as she drove away from the house. She had felt a bit like the bitch Edna when having eased open the front door she indicated to Grandpa that he should enter. How obedient he was, and how sweet of disposition, or that is how you could interpret his passivity. No wonder the girl Lucy was so attached to him. Well, now she had him back and Rosa half regretted giving him up.

She had written a novel once about a woman and her autistic son, drawing out the eerie presence of another human being who lacked all the usual connectors of a human being. Needless to say, she had identified with the child who had become her viewpoint character. Who knew what went on in a mind that had seemingly shut out the world reported by the senses? This gave her the artistic leeway to develop her private version of autism. The story had been told by a child for whom the actions of the story took place behind a screen. A narrative without any internal judgment on the deeds performed—that had to be provided by the reader. It was her favorite novel. It had not been a great success, but then she hadn't expected it to. Once begun she could not have stopped writing the novel out of considerations of commercial expectations.

In the ancient myth of the underworld, after the wraithlike soul survived the terrors of Hades and emerged on the Elysian Fields to enjoy a thousand years of bliss, it must then pass through the waters of forgetfulness, the river Lethe, when all memories of the afterlife were washed away so the soul could be united with another body and begin a new terrestial journey. Alzheimer's was a version of that, except that the soul remained in the same body which could no longer serve its normal purpose.

Everyone suppressed memories of the bad things he had done and admitted only the good. Or, if the bad were admitted, it was only on special terms that neutralized the badness. To this Rosa was an exception, perhaps because so few good things had come her way. Her fans might find that preposterous, her agent and editors would gush about her phenomenal success, but Rosa knew better. Her writing was a transaction with herself carried out in the workroom constructed to facilitate it. What happened to the stories when she sent them off interested her less and less. Her prolific output was a personal need, not the satisfaction of the demands of her readers. To hell with them.

She could imagine that her reaction to Edna's abandoning of Grandpa that fateful night was to the world's treatment of herself. It was a cliche that a writer's capital is amassed in youth and then spent over the course of a career. What happened later could never have the impact of those formative years, and her formative years had been hell. In bringing Edna to justice, she had avenged herself as much as Grandpa.

How unusual such reflections seemed, there had been so little of them of late. Nick was a distraction in the way Grandpa was not. In sex shops there were inflatable dolls for lonely men to mate with, and dildos for the lonely woman. But Nick was not an inflatable doll. None of her male guests had been. When she had rid herself of them it was to return to the solitude she needed in order to release the demons that had taken possession of her as a girl.

Shortly after she arrived home, the metallic clank in the basement began. He had heard her come in. She went to the kitchen and filled a feeding bowl with dog food and took it to the basement. A haggard Nick cried out at the sight of her.

"For the love of God, let me go."

"I took Grandpa home."

His beard did not become him. His eyes were bloodshot and his wrist was raw from constantly beating against the pipe that made a prisoner of him. He listened wild-eyed to her words.

"Good. There's no reason to keep me now. I won't tell, I promise."

"In your situation, promises are worthless."

"Rosa, I swear. Let me go and I will erase everything from my mind."

"We'll see. Eat your dinner."

He had reacted with disgust at the dog food the first time she brought it to him. He said he would starve before he ate it. But now he fell to like an animal, pushing his face into it although he had a free hand he could have used.

"I am going upstairs, Nick. If you persist in making that noise, I will have to beat you."

"Take me with you, Rosa." He looked up from the dish, his face smeared with the wet mash he had been eating. "Take me to your workroom. We'll make love."

He could not know how disgusting he now seemed to her. How long would things have gone on between them if he had not discovered Grandpa? An academic question. A less academic question was what she would do with him.

She took the question with her upstairs, ignoring his cries of agony. The pitch of his screaming rose when she turned off the basement light. She settled in her workroom whose cork

227

walls muffled his despairing howl. She called up on the screen a story she had tried to start, but it held no interest for her. A window appeared indicating that she had e-mail. There was a message from someone named Manfredi. A single word. *Rosebud.*

Rosa deleted it angrily. But the anger gave way to concern. She remembered Earwick's call and his whispering of that word. That had been a challenge and so was this e-mail. But she did not know who Manfredi was. The message indicated that, like Earwick, he had pieced things together and identified her as the custodian of Grandpa. And the executor of Edna. Manfredi must have linked the death of Earwick to her as well.

He must be a policeman. She called police headquarters and asked for Lieutenant Manfredi.

"Captain. Who's calling?"

"Rosebud."

7

They called from downtown to tell him Rosebud had left a message. Told him with a chuckle, it had to be a joke, and how often did they get a chance to taunt Manfredi.

"Did she leave a number?"

The origin of incoming calls was recorded. He jotted down the number he was given, no chuckle now, and said he would wait until they found out the location of the person whose number it was.

"Manfredi, that will take a little time. I'll call you."

"No, I'll wait."

He did not feel suspense. The e-mail ploy had worked. Now he would have her address. He had to consider how to proceed from there. Had Earwick been in this position a week before and underestimated the ingenuity of a woman who had already killed one other person for sure? Manfredi did not propose to make such a mistake. His danger was to overestimate the woman. His only description of her had come from Fred.

"You're kidding."

Fred shook his head. "When she spoke, they had her on a podium and she wore a hat and glasses. Afterward, when I went up to get a book signed, I saw she was the same little troll she had been when she worked for Thompson's."

Fred had not realized he was speaking of the woman who had killed his wife.

"What did you tell Hazel?"

"She wasn't the older woman Nick was having the affair with."

Nick had written a feature story on Rosa Subiaco. Manfredi guessed that she was the woman Nick had blubbered to Fred about. But that was after the first time. Had she fed Nick to the fish too?

"Manfredi? 3306 Columbus."

"Thanks."

"Anything else?"

He hesitated. Earwick had gone solo and didn't live to regret it. Visions of the swat squad descending on the house danced before his mind's eye. He shook his head.

"That's it."

Her MO indicated that she avoided weapons, relying on any means ready to hand. She had not needed one with Edna but Earwick had been struck a terrible blow to the head. Manfredi could not rule out that she was armed. With thought came a way. More lore from Fred helped. Manfredi got in touch with Victor Armitage, director of the public library in Toledo. He drove down there to talk with the man.

He might have been Grandpa before the Alzheimer's hit him.

"Tell me about Rosa Subiaco."

Victor beamed. "A real success story."

"Do you have a corduroy jacket?"

8

Rosa sat in her darkened upstairs bedroom, which gave her a view of the street in front and the alley in back. Her house had been her refuge, but now she felt imprisoned in it, no better off than Nick in the basement. Fleeing had been only fleetingly attractive. She was dealing with the police now and the police could track her down easily. Home turf was better, but not what she would have preferred. Her preferences had ceased to matter.

She had amassed an arsenal, ordering weapons over the web and a lethal rifle lay upon the bed. In her hand she held the gun that had sufficed to subdue Earwick. The plot in which she was embroiled and no longer controlled was coming to its climax. The battle that had been first declared when she as a child was entering a decisive phase. Had her whole life tended to this as its ultimate meaning? Why did it seem so meaningless?

Hours passed and she decided that Manfredi had decided to play cat and mouse with her as she had with Earwick. He would not come tonight. He had all the time in the world. And then she heard the car pull up in front of the house. An ordinary car. And only one. She scampered across the room to look out back, but there was nothing there. Rosa smiled. He was as stupid as Earwick after all.

She snatched up the rifle and floated down the stairs. From the dining room window she looked out at the parked car. Just sitting there. Cat and mouse. Well, the best defense is a surprising offense.

She went into the front hallway and propped the attack rifle in the corner and, gripping the gun, pulled open the front door. And stopped.

The door of the car had opened and someone had started up the walk to the house. My God, it couldn't be. Grandpa had come back. She moved toward him.

"Rosa," he said.

"You can speak."

He was closer now and then she recognized him.

"Victor!"

And then the gun was wrested from her by someone who had come up from behind. She felt the cuffs snap onto her wrist, a tight and painful fit. She turned to face her captor.

"Captain Manfredi, I presume."

Epilogue

Manfredi sat in O'Boyle's with a Guinness before him and the time in which to enjoy it and any number of its successors. He was determined to keep his mind off the events that had so recently reached a climax with the arrest of Rosa Subiaco. An open and shut case, one would have thought, but her expensive imported attorney was conducting a running seminar for the media on the multiple ways in which his client's rights had been violated.

Tell it to Grandpa Yates.

Tell it to Edna Huff and poor old Earwick, fed to the fish by the prolific author whom liposuction had recently reduced to half her former weight. A featured story by Nicholas Byers in the *Fort Elbow Tribune* chronicled the compassionate way in which she had succored the unfortunate Grandfather Yates when his family had abandoned him. From sea to shining sea, Rosa's millions of fans were rising to her support, threatening to converge on Fort Elbow.

Noonan, looking smug, asked Manfredi if he thought Rosa would get off.

"Ask Nick Byers."

Gloria chuckled. Noonan looked puzzled. Portrait of a Missing Person.

Fred Huff slipped into the booth across from Manfredi

and soon the Guinness he had ordered arrived.

"How's Hazel?"

"Nuts."

Manfredi had Theresa so he could match stories with anyone on the irrationality of women. But then men were worthy sons of their mothers. Fred had proposed to Hazel. She had turned him down. In the worst month of his life, he had surpassed all the other salesmen at Thompson's in gross sales.

Lucy was devoting full time to Grandpa, but how long could that last? It was all over with Nick, but there was the devoted friend of her parents hovering in the wings.

"You get any of the lottery money, Fred?"

"Lucy offered me several million."

"And?"

"I'm thinking about it."

What is it like to think over an offer of several million dollars? By the look of Fred, money did not seem the promise of happiness. He would have preferred Hazel and she had turned him down.

"You could buy a bunch of fast food franchises."

Fred looked at Manfredi with a spark of interest in his eye. "Yeah."

There are no happy endings. Manfredi lit a cigarette and inhaled deeply. He had recently had a chest x-ray and his lungs were clear. He read the message on the cigarette package. Perhaps he could engage Rosa's lawyer and sue the tobacco company for false advertisement.

"I suppose I could take the money and retire," Fred murmured.

Manfredi reacted with alarm. "Don't do it! I could tell you stories. Die with your boots on."

"I'd have to buy a pair first."

"You can afford it."

Another round of Guinness arrived, unbidden, and then Alex Schuler joined them.

"How goes the battle, counselor?"

But it is not the battles that matter. Lost or won, they are only episodes in a war whose beginnings are lost in the shadows of the past and which doubtless will continue as long as there are sufficient numbers of poor forked animals to carry it on. Manfredi lit another cigarette, dedicating it to the Surgeon General who showed such touching concern for his well being.